Reviews

"Well written story wit ... *language and a professional's keenness on simplification and comprehension. A must-have in your library if you want your child to start thinking project management automatically! As an author, parent and project management professional, I enjoyed the reading from cover to cover. Thanks Gary!"* - **Fairooz Tamimi, Award Winning Novelist and PMP**

"The Valentine's Day Project Disaster strongly demonstrates that with the right tools and processes students are capable of far more than we expect of them. Project management, people management, and time management are all skills that can be learned and Gary Nelson teaches those skills through engaging characters, situations, and story lines. Young or old, The Valentine's Day Project Disaster is a fun way to learn how to bring an idea to life!" - **Kris Beisel, Director - Educational Alliances, Destination Imagination, Inc.**

"With this book you can make the best Valentine's Day Dance at your school – ever! But watch out for Pimple Pete!" - **Sienna Burns (Age 10)**

"While everyone knows Project Managers should be professionally detached from their stakeholders, it can be really difficult when you are only 12 - and Valentine's Day is involved! The Project Kids face a big challenge in trying to balance delivering a project (Valentine dance), engaging and influencing their stakeholders (a whole school of students, teachers and the principal), and keeping a clear head...all while Cupid is circling above. Important lessons are given for children - and adults, too!" - **Tony van Krieken, PMP, MA**

"Gary's ability to explain projects, project management and key concepts in an easy to understand and interesting way is just amazing. He has figured out the formula to teach crucial life skills to young adults and have them eagerly participate. Soon we will all be asking "What would the project kids do?" - **Stephen Nosal, President Elect, Project Management Institute New York City Chapter**

On previous books in the series:

"This book is outstanding! It teaches us kids that we can make a project out of literally everything we do. I enjoyed reading the book, and can't wait for the next one."
Sofia Triana, Age 10 - 5th grade

"This is a captivating children's story which presents how to plan and execute a project in order to achieve success using basic project management concepts. I would recommend it to anyone, both children and adults, who are interested in learning about project management as a useful life skill."
Agnieszka Krogulec, PMI Poland Chapter

"The Scariest Haunted House Project-Ever is a fun and educational read for children. It puts the practicalities of project management into a tangible format for children to begin to understand. It is a great resource for classroom teaching on the many facets of project management. I would recommend this book to anyone wanting a fun read or to teach their children valuable project management skills." - **Natalie Smith, Year 6-7 Teacher, Puketaha School**

Project Kids Adventures

The Valentine's Day Project Disaster

Gary M. Nelson, PMP

Illustrated by Mathew Frauenstein

With selected artwork by Liam Nelson

Print ISBN-10: 151169758X
Print ISBN-13: 978-1511697583

This is a work of fiction. Names, characters, businesses, places, events and incidents are either the products of the author's imagination or used in a fictitious manner. Any resemblance to actual persons, living or dead, or actual events is purely coincidental.

<u>Safety first!</u> Always use appropriate protective gear when handling tools and materials. Talk to a parent or qualified person for help if you ever need First Aid advice or assistance for any reason.

Dedication

For Lorna - you will always be my Valentine.

For my two youngest sons, Liam (13) & Daniel (12), my sounding boards and story-time reviewers for all the books - you have helped make the Project Kids what they are.

And for everyone who can still remember their first Valentine's dance.

The Valentine's Day Project *Disaster*

Acknowledgements

The project kids are not the only ones to develop and grow throughout the series; Mathew's skills have developed considerably over the past few years, although his skills have always been better than the cartoon style used for the books. However, nothing stands still forever, and we decided to let the project kids do a little 'growing up' through the artwork style used in this book. It was a tough decision, but I hope a good one. I think the new style going forward helps reflect the growing confidence and capabilities of the project kids. Besides, as you hear kids everywhere say, "I'm not a little kid anymore!" Well done Mathew.

Many thanks to my proofreaders, Vicki Burns, Christine Pemberton and Kathleen Hall - I appreciate all you have done to make the book better.

A special thanks to Liam, who is a budding artist in his own right, for the decorations in Chapter 19.

Gary Nelson, PMP

Hamilton, New Zealand

February 14, 2016

Contents

1.	Hasty Decisions	1
2.	I Could Have Said No	9
3.	Pimple Pete	15
4.	Temporary Insanity	23
5.	New Recruits	27
6.	Second Fiddle	37
7.	Sour Grapes	45
8.	Fearless Leader	51
9.	No-Man's Land	63
10.	Behind Enemy Lines	71
11.	Battle Plans	83
12.	Because I Said So	105
13.	Green-Eyed Monster	117
14.	Rumor Has It…	123
15.	Poison Pen	133
16.	One Little Kiss	141

17. Face the Music   149

18. Love Me...Not   159

19. Sweet Revenge   171

20. Just Desserts   181

The Easter Bully Transformation Project   193

The Project Kids Team   195

Glossary   203

Notes for Parents and Teachers   215

I. Hasty Decisions

"What have I done?" moaned Amanda as she sat in the 'reading room' of the tree house on Tuesday afternoon. Actually, it was just the lowest platform of the tree house, where they kept comic books in a plastic container. She leaned across the rope railing, her feet dangling in the air below. The other eight platforms disappeared high into the tree above her.

She sighed and leaned back on her elbows, brushing aside her long brown hair to study the maze of rope ladders and platforms suspended above her head. It was quite impressive really - she had built it all last summer with three of her best friends, Alice, Susan and Becky. *Well, maybe not all on our own*, she sighed. The boys helped after their own tree house got wrecked. All except for her brother Ben, of course, who broke his leg when he'd had a massive tantrum and fallen out of the boys' tree house. Ben had brown hair like Amanda,

1

but Amanda had piercing green eyes instead of brown.

Amanda tried to make out the top-most platform, which was just barely visible from her vantage point. Platform Nine - *her platform*, right at the top of the tree. She allowed herself a small smile before she sat up straight. She glanced at the piece of paper that sat on top of the plastic clip box that served as their comic library.

"It's all *your* fault," she accused the piece of paper.

The paper ignored her.

"Or maybe it was *your* fault first," she said, looking around at the tree house. "If we hadn't done this *first* project, I wouldn't be in this mess!"

She sighed and patted the wooden plank beside her right hand. "Nah, I'm glad we built you. It was a lot of fun, and we've certainly enjoyed using the tree house. It even let me do something better than Ben for a change."

"Who are you talking to?" called a voice from below.

"Who's there?" called Amanda, as she moved to stand up. She walked over to the railing and looked down. "Oh, it's *you,* Tim. What are you doing here?"

"Same as you, I wanted to spend some time in the tree house. I finished my homework for the day, so I decided to come read some comics," Tim replied.

"Although I'm not sure I want to disturb your conversation with the *tree*," Tim shook his head.

Amanda ignored the comment. "Where's Tom?"

Tom was Tim's red-head identical twin brother, and they were almost always found together. They often finished each other's sentences, which was a bit distracting until you got used to it. Tim and Tom were a year younger than Amanda, and still in primary school.

Tim shook his head. "He's still doing his homework. He got in trouble for playing games before he finished his homework yesterday. Now he has to finish *all* of this week's homework *and* wash the dishes after dinner, so it's just me this time," said Tim as he began climbing the rope ladder.

Amanda waited for Tim to reach the top of the ladder and make his way over to the reading platform.

"So how are you doing, anyway? How's middle school?" asked Tim.

Amanda shrugged. "Middle school's OK I guess. I'm getting used to it."

"Aaaand - how is *Oliver?*" he asked.

Amanda blushed. "Um, well he's fine, I guess. Like I'd really know."

"Aw c'mon, you used to say you hated him, but from what I hear it's not that way anymore," said

Tim, grinning. "I don't even go to the same *school* as you anymore, and that's all I hear about these days!"

Amanda's blush turned even redder. "Umm, well, umm, it's really none of your business, anyway."

"So you *didn't* hold his hand?" asked Tim, eyebrows raised.

"Umm, yes, well, maybe but, but…"

"But *what?* So you like him now, *big deal.*" Tim shrugged. "People change their minds all the time. Even about people like Oliver."

"***What's wrong with Olly?***" demanded Amanda.

"**Whoah!** I think all that hair pulling must have killed some of your brain cells. Or did you forget that part?" asked Tim, taking a careful step back.

Amanda waved her hands in the air. "Oh that, that was nothing. He said he did that because he wanted to get my attention, and he was nervous about talking to me. You *do* know boys can be real stupid sometimes, right?" said Amanda, left eyebrow raised.

Tim shrugged. "Sure, all kinds of people can act stupid. Not *just* boys," replied Tim.

"Gahhh!" muttered Amanda. "I don't know which is worse - arguing about how stupid people are, or that!" she pointed to the piece of paper on the plastic container.

4

The Valentine's Day Project *Disaster*

Tim bent over to pick it up.

"*Don't touch that!*" yelled Amanda.

"Too late," said Tim as he started to read the sheet of paper. Amanda's shoulders slumped.

"So what's the problem?" asked Tim after he finished reading the page and set it back down on the plastic container.

Amanda sat down heavily on the edge of the platform. Tim sat down beside her and swung his legs back and forth, unconsciously matching her rhythm.

Amanda sat quietly for nearly a minute before she replied. "You remember the last project, the Science Fair thing with the maze?" Amanda studied the laces on her shoes as her feet swung back and forth.

"Yup," nodded Tim. "I was part of the experiment. That was cool driving the robot around."

Amanda took a deep breath. "Uh-huh. *Well*, after Christmas break, our principal, Ms. Moldiva, came to my math class to see me. She asked me to come out into the hallway for a moment. At first I thought I was in *trouble* or something..." she paused, studying her laces once more, "...but I had no idea how much trouble!"

"I mean, *why me?* Just because we did a few good projects this year, she picked on *me*." Amanda sighed. "First, she said she wanted to personally congratulate me on the Science Fair project, which felt *pretty good*, you know?"

"And then, then she pulled out *this*," Amanda picked up the piece of paper and shook it. "She *set me up*, I swear! How could I say *no* after all the nice things she said?"

Tim patted Amanda on the shoulder. "It won't be that bad," he said. "You'll get help, and it'll be fine. You'll see."

Amanda looked sideways at Tim, unconvinced. "I'm going to need a *lot* of help. So - are you going to help me again this time?"

Tim patted her shoulder as he stood up, shaking his head. "Nah, I don't know... that's really a *middle school* thing, and like it or not, us boys are still in primary school. I don't know how it could possibly work, especially with something like *that*."

Tim called out again as he climbed down the ladder. "But don't worry; I'm sure you'll get *plenty* of help. Good luck!"

"*Thanks for nothing*," muttered Amanda, crumpling up the piece of paper.

When the sound of Tim walking through the forest had faded away, Amanda slowly opened up the wad of paper and smoothed it out on the wooden planks.

Those awful words were still there, unchanged by the crumpling of the paper.

The Valentine's Day Project *Disaster*

In large, bold print was printed:

Organizer needed for the Valentine's Day school dance.

Amanda shuddered and stuffed the paper into her pocket. "This is going to be a *disaster!*"

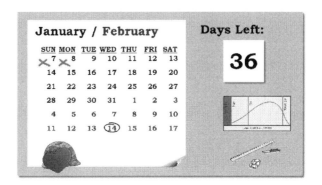

Hasty Decisions

2. I Could Have Said No

Why did I say yes to this? Amanda wondered the next morning in class.

The problem with success is that people expect more from you, she frowned. *I must have been crazy! Run a couple of good projects, and now they want me to do this?*

I Could Have Said No

She stared hard at the crumpled piece of paper sitting face-down on the desk in front of her, hoping it would just go away.

She cautiously poked at it again with the end of her pencil, like it was a bomb about to go off. She flicked at the crumpled edge of the paper, those terrible words hidden just out of sight, taunting her.

Finally, she could take it no more. She put down the pencil and grasped the paper with shaking hands. *Why did I agree to run this project? What do I know about any of this stuff, anyway? Yes, no problem, Ms. Moldiva. Sure! It'll be fun!*

"What's up?" asked Becky as she slid into the seat next to Amanda.

Amanda dropped the pencil onto her desk and turned to face Becky. "I can't believe I agreed to organize the Valentine's Day Dance. I mean, we just got back from Christmas break, which was like, you know, *really* busy, and before that was the Science Fair and before that the Haunted House. It never seems to end, you know? What I really need is a *break* and..."

Becky shook her head, her long brown hair promptly falling over her face. She brushed it back behind her ears and stared at Amanda with deep brown eyes. "You're just coming up with excuses. You know you'll be *great* at it. That *we* will all be great at it, because of course Susan and I will help you."

"Help with what?" asked Susan, as she took a seat behind Amanda. Her blonde pigtails bobbed up and down as she slid her bag under her seat. She looked over Amanda's shoulder at the crumpled paper. "Oh, OK, right, of course...gee, thanks Becky for volunteering me. You know what I think about that mushy stuff..."

Amanda twisted around in her seat, frowning. "So what, now you're **not** going to help?"

"**What?** No, I mean *yes*, but it is always polite to be *asked first*, you know?" said Susan, flustered. "Of course we will help, we're a team. I just don't like being volun*told*, you know? I would have offered to help anyway." Susan tugged at her hair. "It's what friends do."

Amanda turned halfway in her seat so she could see both Becky and Susan. "So that's the start of it then, the three amigas. But something this big is going to take a lot more help. I mean just blowing up the balloons alone - I am already getting out of breath thinking about it. And then there are all of the streamers and the decorations and the food and drinks and tables and chairs and the lights and..." Amanda paused, face flushed and out of breath.

"...And the music?" suggested Becky.

"**Right!** And the *music*, and a hundred or so other things that I *just don't know about* that will cause all of this to be one *horrible, miserable, awful disaster*, and when it all goes wrong, it will be **my fault!**"

I Could Have Said No

Amanda slumped back into her chair in despair. "How are we possibly going to do this - this *thing?*"

Becky and Susan exchanged glances. It wasn't often that Amanda looked this uncertain about things. She was usually much more 'in charge'.

"Aww, we'll figure it out. Besides, it's not always about *what you know*," said Becky.

"Right! Sometimes it's about *who you know*," said Susan. "We just have to ask someone who has done this before. They can just tell us what needs to be done, and then we'll do it!"

Amanda looked up slowly and was greeted by two forced grins. "I guess so…" she paused, "…but fix your faces 'cos those smiles aren't fooling anyone!" said Amanda.

"If you don't know, ask!" said Becky. "That's what you did with your dad for our other projects."

Amanda looked down at her desk. "I don't think he can help with something like this. He's like, you know, *old*. They probably never even invented Valentine's Day when he was our age."

Becky and Susan just nodded. Becky didn't think her parents were *quite* that old, but she wasn't about to argue with Amanda now that she was starting to act more normal again.

"OK, at recess we'll go find out who organized the dance last year, and then grill them with a hundred questions," said Amanda.

12

The Valentine's Day Project *Disaster*

"I'll bring the paper and pencils," offered Susan.

"I'll think up some good questions," offered Becky.

"At recess then," declared Amanda, and then carefully folded up the piece of paper and stuck it in her pocket.

I Could Have Said No

3. Pimple Pete

Finding out 'who' they needed to know turned out to be quite difficult. Half of the kids turned and walked away when they heard the words 'Valentine's Dance'. The other half just pretended to ignore them. After fifteen minutes they finally found someone who would actually *talk* to them.

"Oh, you want to talk to **Pimple Pete**," said a blonde eighth grader. "He organized it last year.

Pimple Pete

That's probably why most of the kids were ignoring you - well, at least the eighth graders. Word gets around. I wouldn't be surprised if the entire school had heard about it by now."

"Heard about what?" asked Amanda, getting annoyed.

"Heard about how Pete ran the Valentine's Day Dance last year. He would probably have run it again this year, but apparently it's just a grade seven thing to run it, you know? Some dumb idea the old principal had about encouraging the younger kids to *expand their horizons*. I am surprised you volunteered to do it. Moldiva must have suckered you in real good in order to convince you to coordinate that train wreck," said the eighth grader.

Amanda's face had gone pale. "What do you mean, *train wreck?*"

Susan and Becky moved closer to Amanda. She didn't look well, and they wanted to be able to catch her if she fainted.

"I mean, like almost nobody came, except the ones who organized it. And they were only there because Pete *made them* come. He was so pushy and a bully about it that, yeah sure, they had the gym decorated and all that, but it wasn't exactly what I would call *fun*, you know?"

Amanda stood up straight and cocked her jaw. "Well, the *real* problem was that some *stupid boy*

16

organized it, that's what. You just wait and see, they're going to have a fun time, whether they like it or not!" declared Amanda.

The eighth grader gave her an odd look. "You know, you almost sounded like Pete did last year, when he heard about the dance the year before, except *that one* was run by a *girl*."

Amanda stepped back, stunned. "I'm nothing like Pete, whoever he is. I mean, *who does he think he is?* And why do you keep calling him *Pimple Pete*, anyway?"

"Because I have a lot of pimples," came a voice from right behind Amanda. Pete had walked up quietly behind her while she was ranting.

Pete came around to stand beside the eighth grader. "As you can clearly see, it's a pain turning thirteen. But just wait - it'll be your turn soon. And as for *who I am...*" he paused, and gave Amanda a cold, appraising look.

"*I* am Peter Johansen, and I'm the person who will be able to tell you all about the stuff we did last year, and how to run the Valentine's Dance. Sure, it may not have been well attended, but I would like to think we learned a thing or two from it. If I was able to do it again this year, it would be much better, of course. But ...I didn't get asked, *you* did - and that means that I'm only here to *advise* you," Pete smirked. "As long as you treat me nicely and say *pretty please*, that is."

Pimple Pete

Amanda stood there staring at him, mouth hanging open.

"Otherwise, you're on your own, New Girl," Pete said, with a twisted grin.

"*All on your own...*" he called over his shoulder as he walked away with the eighth grader.

"Um, Amanda, my name is **Amanda!**" she called out after him. "**And I need some help!**"

"You didn't say *pretty please*," yelled Pete, shaking his head.

"Pretty..." Amanda gritted her teeth. "***Pretty Please!!***"

Amanda could hear Pete laugh as he yelled back. "Good enough. Come see me behind the gym after school."

Amanda's shoulders slumped, and it looked like she was going to crumple up completely. Becky put her hand on Amanda's shoulder to steady her.

"I'm *fine*, I'll be fine," muttered Amanda. "But this is going to be much more difficult than I thought."

The bell rang and the three girls quickly crunched through the gravel as they ran to their next class.

"Now, I'm more determined than ever to make sure this is the *best* Valentine's Dance this school has ever seen. I mean, how could it be possibly *worse* than whatever *Pimple Pete* put together?"

The Valentine's Day Project *Disaster*

The three girls waited behind the gymnasium after school. They had been waiting for over ten minutes and were about to leave when Pete and a couple of other boys came around the corner.

"See, guys? I knew she'd be there, even if we showed up late. I mean, anyone who's *dumb* enough to volunteer to run the dance has to be *desperate* for help, right Chip?" said Pete with a smirk to the blonde, blue eyed boy on his left.

"You mean like you were last year, when you had to organize the dance?" asked Chip, winking.

"**Yes!** I mean *no*, not exactly like that. I just needed a few pointers, that's all," growled Pete.

"No, I think you needed a lot *more* than a little bit of help last year". Todd had short, wavy brown hair and deep brown eyes.

"*Whatever*," waved Pete dismissively. "The point is that she needs help, and probably a lot more than we did, because she's *just* a girl."

Susan jumped in first. "What do you mean, *just a girl?*"

"We didn't *need* any girls on our committee last year," said Pete.

"That's probably why it was such a mess," muttered Becky under her breath.

Pimple Pete

"**Boys! Girls!**" yelled Amanda. "Settle down. We are here to learn from last year's Valentine's Dance committee," said Amanda, fixing her glare on Pete. "And we are *most certainly not desperate.* In fact, I think the most important thing we may learn today is *what not to* do when running a school dance."

"That remains to be seen," replied Pete, warily. "Maybe we won't tell you *everything* we know."

"Doesn't matter, we'll just fill in the gaps," said Becky.

"Maybe I'll *lie* about parts of it," snapped Pete.

"It seems your friends probably won't let you," said Susan. "We've seen that already."

Pete threw his hands up in the air. "Well! We had better get started, seeing you are all chums already."

Together the six children walked over to the nearest picnic table and sat down, boys on one side and girls on the other. Amanda stared at Pete, who sat directly across from her in the center. Susan nodded at Todd. Becky smiled shyly at Chip.

"Chip's a cool name," said Amanda.

"Actually it's Charles, but I prefer to be called Chip," he shrugged. "It's just a nickname, I think Charles sounds too stuffy."

The Valentine's Day Project *Disaster*

Susan pulled out a pad of paper and two pencils. She wrote 'Valentine's Dance' at the top of the page then sat ready, her pencil poised to write.

"Now then!" said Amanda, clearing her throat. "Tell us what it takes to run a Valentine's Dance, and don't leave anything out - the good *or* the bad. We need to hear it all!"

By the time they had finished, the sun had moved a fair way around the sky and their picnic table was now in shadow. Susan had fifteen pages of hand-written notes, and her hand was getting sore.

The six children stood up, and Amanda held out her hand.

Pete stared at it suspiciously. "What's that?"

"My hand, dummy. I wanted to thank you for all your help," said Amanda.

"Uh-huh, well, that's all you are going to get, so make the most of it," said Pete, cautiously shaking her hand. "After this, you're *on your own.*"

Todd and Chip stretched and yawned as the children walked towards the front of the school.

"I'd be happy to help," Todd whispered to Susan as they walked side by side, crunching through the gravel.

Susan mouthed a quiet 'thank you' so that Pete wouldn't notice.

Pimple Pete

"I'll tell you my ideas later," Chip whispered to Becky. "Come find me at recess some time."

Becky nodded.

Amanda and Pete walked in silence all the way to the front gate. After they passed through the gate, Amanda and the girls turned right. Chip and Todd crossed the road together. Pimple Pete turned left and walked home, alone.

4. Temporary Insanity

"I can't believe they suckered you into doing it," said Ben as he helped Amanda set the table. "I mean, that sounds like some scary-big project, running a *whole school dance*. Especially a *Valentine's Day* Dance. You girls wrote down, what, like *ten pages* of stuff you had to do? That's impossible!"

January / February

SUN	MON	TUE	WED	THU	FRI	SAT
7	8	9	10	11	12	13
14	15	16	17	18	19	20
21	22	23	24	25	26	27
28	29	30	31	1	2	3
4	5	6	7	8	9	10
11	12	13	(14)	15	16	17

Days Left:

34

Temporary Insanity

Amanda sighed and adjusted the knife she had just put down so it was sitting parallel with the fork on the other side of the plate. She looked up at her brother and shrugged. "Fifteen pages, but Susan writes big. Besides, *I* don't really know why I agreed to it either. You think I can plead *temporary insanity* and get out of the whole thing?"

Ben shrugged. "If you were still in primary school, maybe. But if you ask me, most of those kids in your school are half nuts anyway, so it would never work," Ben frowned. "I mean, now you're hanging out with *Oliver*, and he used to pull your hair. You *really hated him*, and that was the main reason I asked him to be my partner for the Halloween project."

Amanda stuck out her tongue. "Oh, I don't know, he's not that bad once you get to know him. Plus, he *is* kind of cute."

Ben pretended to vomit. "*See what I mean? Crazy*, the whole lot of you. There's no way you could get out of it by pleading temporary insanity. You're just plain nuts all the time now."

"Just wait, it'll be your turn next year, and then *you'll* be crazy too," smiled Amanda.

"Not if I fail all my grades, they might keep me in primary school. It might be worth it - I kind of like being the 'big' kid at school," said Ben.

"*Now* who's crazy?" Amanda shook her head. "Mom and Dad would *kill you* if you tried a stunt like that. Nope, you are *doomed* to come to middle school next year, just like me."

Ben just grunted and set down the last plate on the table. "We'll see. We'll see."

"She's in *way* over her head," Ben said, poking at an ant with a stick. He was sitting at the picnic table in the playground with James, Tim and Tom. They had a few minutes before the first school bell rang, but Ben felt like he needed to talk for a change rather than have a go on the swings.

"Yeah, she told me all about it in the tree house the other day," said Tim. "Sounds like a big job. She even asked *me* if I would help."

Ben looked up from the ant and stared at Tim. "So what did you say?"

"Well, I told her that it was really a *middle school* thing," said Tim, staring down at the table. "It's not something I felt comfortable with, you know? If it was something like another tree house, of course I would help, but this is a *dance* we are talking about." He shuddered. "I don't even know *how* to dance."

James shook his head. "Not something I would want to help with, either." He pushed a few fingers

25

through his tangled mop of blonde hair to make sure it was still suitably messy.

"Nope, not interested," said Tom.

"I don't know…it sounds strange, but I'm worried about her," said Ben, fixing his gaze back on the ground. The ant had disappeared into a forest of grass. Ben tossed the stick out onto the gravel.

Tim and Tom exchanged glances.

Ben worried about Amanda? He could barely stand his older sister. It's got to be bad, thought Tim.

"Oh, I don't know…" said James, shifting his feet uncomfortably. "I'm sure she'll be just fine."

Tom nodded, followed closely by Tim.

"I mean, she's got Susan and Becky to help, she'll figure it out," said Tom, trying to convince himself.

"Yeah, she doesn't need us at all," said Tim, not believing a single word.

5. New Recruits

"Right then, well I guess we'd better get started, a whole weekend is gone already," sighed Amanda as she took a seat at her kitchen table and picked up a pencil. Her eyes wandered randomly around the table until they landed on the stack of papers to her left. With a small moan, she lifted a blank piece of paper from the stack and placed it in front of her.

New Recruits

"Are you OK?" asked Becky, watching Amanda closely. "You seemed pretty out of it today at school."

"Hum? What? Oh, sure, just another project, just another Monday, no problem," shrugged Amanda, breaking the tip of the pencil on the sheet of paper.

"Like I said, we need to go over the stuff we need to do for every project," said Amanda, starting to draw with the broken pencil. She appeared confused when nothing showed up on the paper, other than some dents and small slivers of wood.

"You are most definitely *not all right*," said Susan, taking away Amanda's pencil. "Becky and I can get started, we know what to do. You just take a break for now, OK?"

"Uhhh, sure," said Amanda, getting up unsteadily from the table. "I'll just go outside for a bit, might clear my head."

"Sounds like a plan. Don't worry, we'll save you some stuff to do," joked Becky, but Susan shot her a warning glance.

"See you in a bit," said Susan, watching Amanda walk down the stairs and go out the front door.

She waited until she heard the door close before she spoke. "Amanda's really messed up. I'm worried."

Becky tried to smile, but her face fell. "Yeah, I'm worried too. This is *not* like her at all."

"Well, like it or not, we have a dance to deliver, whether *she* can do it or not," declared Susan.

"So... let's review the basic steps of a project, to get our brains working properly. The main stages of any project are **Think**, **Plan**, **Do** and **Finish Up**, with the **Lead, Check & Correct** part happening throughout the project."

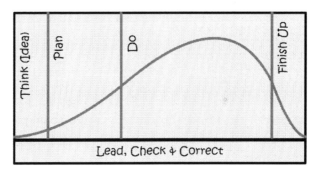

"No matter how big a project or a problem seems, we can start to break it down into smaller, more manageable pieces. They can be pretty simple, like our first project, the tree house."

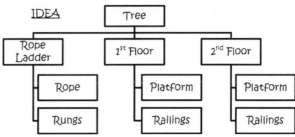

"They can also be more complicated, like the Haunted House or the Science Fair project."

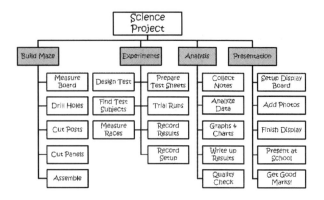

"The key thing is to ask lots of **questions**, so we know as much as possible for our planning. But even if we don't have answers to all of the questions yet, we can tackle them when we need to."

"When we get a big picture view of what needs to happen, then we will figure out what has to happen first, next and so on - these are our *dependencies*, which we draw with arrows between bubbles. Sometimes a bubble, or **task**, can have several dependencies, which we saw on the Haunted House and the Science Fair projects."

The Valentine's Day Project *Disaster*

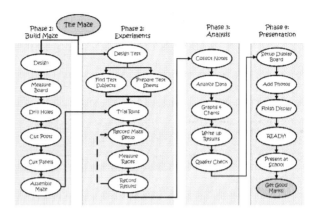

"When we have all of that worked out on paper, the big, scary project is not really that scary at all. Well, at least until you figure out how much effort it is going to take to get stuff done. But even then, if we know that, we can ask for help with certain parts. That way, it's not so overwhelming. That's what Amanda's problem is, I think," said Susan.

"*What is my problem, exactly?*" demanded Amanda, standing in the kitchen doorway. Susan and Becky had been so absorbed they hadn't heard Amanda come up the stairs.

"Um, ahh, it's not that you have a *problem*, exactly…" mumbled Susan.

"It's just that you seem a bit, you know, **overwhelmed** by it all. Like you forgot that you had *friends* to help, and how to approach projects so they don't seem that big or scary," said Becky.

New Recruits

"*Oh really?*" asked Amanda. "Well, I've solved that problem. I brought *reinforcements*. They were just walking by the house, so I asked them to come in."

"Who is it? Tim? Tom? ...James?" Becky asked hopefully as she craned her neck to try and see behind Amanda. The bright sun shining through the window above the front doorway made her squint.

"Nah, we don't need those *little schoolers* anymore. I brought something *better*," said Amanda, stepping aside with a flourish. "I brought *experts*."

From behind Amanda, three figures walked up the steps, silhouetted by the bright sunlight streaming through the window.

"Oh, it's *you*," said Susan, as Todd took a seat at the table.

"Hi Chip," said Becky.

Olly came into the kitchen last, holding Amanda's hand.

"Say that again," prompted Todd. "**Think**, **plan**, *what*?"

"**Think**, **Plan**, **Do**, **Finish Up**," repeated Susan, exasperated. "*See?* Look at these diagrams. I tell you, this is how we need to do it!"

"So this will help us do what, exactly?" asked Chip. "I mean last year, we just got on with things, put up some balloons and stuff, and we had a dance."

"And see what happened when you tried *that*," said Susan. "From what we hear, it was *horrible*. We need to go through *this stuff* to make sure we do it better than you and Pete did last time."

"Uh yeah, maybe..." said Todd, crossing his arms over his chest and leaning back in his chair. "But hey, I mean, we did *fine*. Some people came and everything. There was *music*, there was *dancing,* there was *food*. What else do you need?"

"Maybe we just need to try harder this time," said Chip. "What do you think, Olly?"

Oliver let go of Amanda's hand and sat up straight. "Um, what? How should I know, I wasn't there last year. Why don't you just do what the girls say? It seemed to work for them before."

"Yeah, listen to Olly," said Susan, thrusting several sheets of paper in front of the boys. "See? You need to be *organized* and *simplify* things, so it's easier and you don't forget to do stuff."

"We forgot the soft drinks last year," said Chip, cheeks reddening.

"You see? *Exactly* my point!" declared Susan, who crossed her arms and leaned back in her chair.

Todd leaned forward and shuffled through the diagrams and lists. "I don't know, it's just a bunch of bubbles and lines, and some squiggle drawings. Doesn't look very *organized* to me," he said, frowning.

Chip slid a couple sheets of paper in front of him and began to read them closely. "Hmmm, maybe… I kind of get it, but I think maybe you need to explain it again."

Susan took a deep breath. "I *already* explained it," she gritted her teeth. "It's not that *hard*, you know. I mean, even my *little brother* understands this stuff. And -"

Becky interrupted before Susan could launch into another tirade. "We would be happy to explain it again. Like Susan said, it's not that complicated, once you use it a little bit. Maybe it just requires you to think a bit differently."

"**What**, like a *girl?*" sputtered Todd as he got up from the table. He was halfway to the kitchen doorway when he turned and looked at Chip. "So, are you coming or what?"

Chip started to open his mouth, looked at Becky and shrugged. He slowly got up and stood with Todd at the kitchen doorway.

"There's no way I want to help if it means I have to **think like you**," growled Todd. "I mean, all you've done so far is **insult us**, just like Pete did last year. I've had enough of that, and I don't have to take it anymore!"

The girls stared, open mouthed.

34

"We are **not** like that! **You take that back!**" yelled Susan, cheeks even redder.

Chip just shrugged and said, "Sorry, Becky," as he turned to follow Todd down the stairs.

"Go on and stay if you like, Olly," Todd called back up the stairs. "Looks like those girls have brainwashed you already. Good luck, you'll need it!"

With that, the front door slammed and the house fell quiet.

Oliver finally broke the silence. "Um, so, when's lunch? I'm *starving!*"

New Recruits

6. Second Fiddle

"So *now* what are we going to do?" asked Susan at lunch the next day. The girls were sitting at the picnic table behind the gym, eating sandwiches.

"I don't know, we can just throw something together and hope it works," shrugged Amanda. "I mean, we could always do it *their way*. It's not like many people would show up anyway. So if it's a failure,

37

there won't be many people around to witness it."
Amanda's gaze dropped onto the table.

"I can't believe you just said that," said Becky.
"*Amanda* not wanting to plan? That's just crazy
talk."

At the word 'crazy', Amanda looked up sharply.
"Don't *say that word*, don't *ever* say that word," she
said. "That sounds just like something Ben would
say."

"Aw, it was just a figure of speech," said Becky.

"Well, maybe I *am* crazy," mumbled Amanda.

"No, you're not crazy...but maybe you are a *little*
crazy if you think some dumb *dance* can beat you,"
said Susan. "We just need to put a good plan
together, and get a few more people to help."

"Yeah, so how is that going, then?" sneered
Amanda. "After our *failure* of a planning meeting
where all the *experts* walked out, we all agreed to
go and try to find some other volunteers around the
school. How many people have you got, Becky?"

Becky shifted uncomfortably. "Um, nobody so far."

"And how many people did you ask?"

"Ah, maybe thirty…or forty?" replied Becky.

"Huh," said Amanda. "I asked about fifty, and came
up with a goose egg."

Susan looked at Amanda, eyebrow raised.

"That means *zero*. And how about you, Susan? You seem to know almost everybody in school, so how many people did you get?" asked Amanda, staring at Susan.

Susan sat there for a few moments in silence. She suddenly seemed *extremely* interested in the laces on her left shoe.

"Susan, helloo? Susan," prompted Amanda.

"Um, well, maybe *one* to start with," said Susan. "But -"

"But what?" demanded Amanda, getting annoyed.

"There was a *condition*," sighed Susan.

"So, what was it?" asked Amanda.

"Um, well, he wanted *kisses*..." began Susan.

"*What?!?*" yelled Amanda, causing two birds to leave their perch in a nearby tree. "*Kisses?*"

Amanda took a few breaths, gathering her composure. "So, well, *did you?*"

"Did I *what?*" asked Susan.

"*Kiss him!*" said Amanda, hissing out the words.

Susan looked away, cheeks turning red. "Ah, well, no, you see..."

"*Why didn't you kiss him?* You *know* we need the help. We are getting *desperate!* Nobody else wants to help, the dance is just over a month away, and all you had to do was give this twerp a *little, stupid kiss*, and we would have had more help!"

Susan turned to face her friends with a grim smile. "Um, that's not it, exactly. He wants kiss*es*, not *a kiss*. And he wants them from *each of us*."

"**Oh**," said Amanda, stunned.

"**Oh**," said Becky. "So, what's the matter with him anyway? Is his face all covered in pimples or something?"

"No, it **can't** be Pimple Pete, *just say it isn't **him**...*" moaned Amanda.

Susan shook her head, unable to control her smile anymore. "No pimples yet, that I could see. Actually, he's kind of cute, in his own way."

"So..." began Becky.

"...What does he want then?" sighed Amanda, throwing her hands up.

"Well, he wants kisses, **Hershey's Kisses**, a bag each from Becky and me, and **two** from *you*, Amanda," said Susan. "He says he loves chocolate."

"**What?**" said Amanda, turning red. "**What?** You make us think some *little snot* wants to kiss all of us girls? You think that's funny?"

"Well, actually..." began Susan, giggling.

"Well, I guess it is *kind of* funny," said Becky, poking Susan in the arm. "A *little bit* funny, maybe."

"Well, *I* certainly don't think so," said Amanda. "So who is this *twerp* anyway? Do I know him?"

"Yes, you do. In fact, you know him *really well*," smiled Susan.

"Ohhhh," said Amanda, with a hint of a smile. "Is it Olly, just playing some kind of joke?"

"Nope, someone you know *even better* than that," grinned Susan.

Amanda's face fell. "Um, so who then? I can't think of anyone else."

Susan's grin grew even wider. "Ben."

Amanda looked confused. "What, that tall kid in science class?"

"No, silly, *your brother*. James talked to me about it last night. The boys know that we need help, and we can't find anyone else in our school," said Susan. "And all it will cost us is a few pieces of chocolate!"

"Hmmmm," said Amanda. "Hmmmmmm…"

"We *could* make it work, we know they can work well with us on projects," said Becky.

Amanda looked across the school yard, towards the fence that divided the middle school and her brother's school. "What about Alice? Did you ask her?"

"Not yet, but I will tonight, if we all agree that the boys can help," said Susan.

"Aww, heck, why not. It's not like we have helpers coming out of the woodwork on this side of the fence. It could be worse!" said Amanda.

"Us three, Alice, Ben, Tim, Tom, James - and Olly," confirmed Amanda. "Nine of us will make a good team."

Becky cleared her throat. "Um, Amanda, *about Olly...*"

Amanda turned to glare at Becky. "**What** about my Olly?"

Susan coughed. "It's well, just that Oliver seems to be a bit of a *distraction* for you at the moment. Becky and I were talking about it, and we agreed..." she paused, "...we *agreed* that it might be best if you just *invite* Oliver to the dance, and *not* have him on the team."

"Yeah, the other day when you two were sitting together, it was like he somehow sucked all the brain cells out of your head. Susan and I had to do all the work. Oliver ate lunch, but he didn't actually *contribute* to the planning, not really," said Becky.

Amanda was speechless. She looked back and forth between Susan and Becky, her mouth slowly working, but no sounds came out.

Finally, she took a big gulp of air. "So, you both *agree on this then?*"

The girls nodded.

"So you think the best idea is to *cut Oliver out of our team*. **Oliver**, who loaned us his mouse for the Science Fair project. **Oliver**, whose mouse we maybe killed by overfeeding him pickles. **Oliver**, who I really, really..." her voice fell to a whisper, "...*who I really, really like*."

With that, Amanda stuffed her half-eaten sandwich back into its plastic wrapper, and jammed it into her lunch bag. She closed up the bag and stood up from the table.

"Well, that's it," Amanda declared.

"What's what?" asked Becky.

"You drew a line, and I've made up my mind. I am going to be having lunch with *my Olly* from now on," said Amanda as she started to walk across the playground.

She was halfway to the bench where Oliver sat with a few of his friends when she turned and yelled back "**Good luck with *your* project. *You'll need it!***"

Susan smacked her palm on her forehead. "What is it with her family? Why can't we *ever* get both her and Ben working together on the same project?"

Second Fiddle

"Um, well we kind of did, once - the test subject thing with the Science Fair project..." offered Becky.

"No, that's not the same," sighed Susan. "He didn't actually help *do* the project; he was just a test subject, something to measure in the experiment."

"I don't think that *Ben* is the real problem, anyway. Not this time," said Becky, staring at Amanda, who had just sat down beside Oliver and pulled the mangled sandwich out of her lunch bag.

Oliver offered Amanda a sip from his juice box.

"No, *Ben's* not the problem at all," sighed Becky.

7. Sour Grapes

"So let me get this straight," said James as they sat around Ben's kitchen table.

A fresh plate of warm cookies sat in the middle of the table. There were eight small plates and cups; however Amanda's absence was obvious from the untouched cookie cooling on her plate.

Sour Grapes

"Moldiva asked *Amanda* to do this dance. *Amanda* enlisted you two to help, and now *all of us boys, plus Alice* are helping, but *Amanda* has left the project? She's off somewhere with Oliver?" said James, pushing his fingers through his untidy mop of hair.

"That's right," nodded Becky.

"Sounds real easy, then," snorted James.

Susan leaned forward, a hopeful look in her eyes. "Really? You've got ideas already? That's great!"

"Yeah, real easy. Like just *give up and go home*. It's *Amanda's* problem after all. You two just got sucked into it. This is one reason why we boys never wanted to get involved in the first place. Dances mean *trouble*. Especially *Valentine's Dances*. I hear people start out as friends on dances, then things get messed up, somebody holds someone's hand, maybe somebody gets a kiss, then - BAM! It's all over," said James, waving his hands in the air.

"I heard about it from another school, it was *horrible*. Two best friends don't even speak to each other anymore. I mean, look at this! Amanda started it all, and she's gone, probably not talking to any of us ever again, 'cos she's hanging out with Oliver. What a *mess*," James shook his head.

"***Who's not talking to who?***" asked Amanda, as she slid into the empty chair and took a bite out of a cookie.

"Um, ah, well - you?" said James. "What are *you* doing back here?"

"This is the Valentine's Dance project planning meeting, right?" asked Amanda, wiping a crumb off her lip. "I mean, this *is my project*, right? You even said so, just before."

"What do you want?" demanded Susan, glaring at Amanda. "First, you get us to help, then you abandon us for Oliver, and leave all of this dance up to Becky, me and the rest! What's up with that?" she fumed.

Amanda smiled and waved her right hand airily. "Ah, well, sorry about that. I just wasn't thinking straight for a bit. I'm all good now, ready to get working on the project," she nodded.

Becky wasn't having any of it. "You made it *very clear* that you were *done* with this dance, and you didn't want to do it. What if *we* don't want *you* on this project anymore?"

"I um, well - what do you mean, *you might not want me?*" gasped Amanda. "***How could you say that?***"

"Well, look at it this way. The whole way along you've been hot and cold, a bouncing nut-case, either really gung-ho, or ready to crumple into a heap," sighed Becky. "We just don't know what you're going to do from moment to moment, and we need someone who is *reliable* and *predictable* running this project."

Sour Grapes

"Yeah, and we think it's probably because of Oliver. Your brains must be in your hands, because every time he holds them, you can't think straight," said Susan. "He must be squishing them or something."

Amanda looked around the table at her friends - or at least, the people who *had* been her friends. "Do you all think that?"

Seven heads slowly nodded.

"Oh - I see. *I see*," she put her head in her hands and started to cry. "*What will I do now?*"

"Hold up, what's going on?" asked Tim. "We still like you, you know."

"I- I know, at least I guess so," Amanda sniffed. "It's just, you see, Oliver said we couldn't hang out anymore."

"*What? That pig!*" said Susan. "Why would he do that?"

Amanda looked up, eyes red. "*Because of you. Because of this - this project*. He said I needed to *focus*. I told him everything, what I said to you the other day about leaving the project," she sniffed.

"He said I *promised* Ms. Moldiva I would do the dance, so I *have to do it*. He said he doesn't want to be responsible for the dance failing. He said I need to work hard on this project with all of you," she sniffed again.

"So..." said Amanda, taking a ragged breath, "...he said I can't spend any time with him right now. I need to be *here* - working with you. And he made me - *he made me promise.*"

"Exactly *what* did he make you promise?" asked Becky, warily.

A small smile crept onto Amanda's lips. "He made me *promise* that he would get to be the first one in line to buy a ticket. No, actually, *two* tickets - one for him, and one for me."

"*But* that will only happen if we manage to pull this thing off," she said, sitting straight in her chair and wiping her nose on the side of her hand.

"**So**, *can* I come back to the project? *Please?* I don't even have to lead it, I just want to help, however I can," said Amanda, a hopeful look on her face.

"You know, I think I like Oliver even more than I used to," said Ben, patting Amanda on the arm. "It's OK with me."

One by one, the other children got up and patted Amanda on the back, or gave her a hug.

Alice was the last to hug Amanda. "Welcome back. You know, I think *I* like him too. And he's *brave*, you know, letting you go until the Valentine's Dance. And you are brave too, of course."

Sour Grapes

Amanda leaned her head back to look up at Alice, confused. "Why is he brave? And why exactly I am *I* brave?"

"Because…" said Alice, smoothing out her long black hair as she walked back to her chair, "…*anything* can happen when Valentine's Day is involved. *Anything!*"

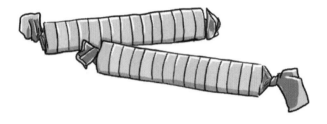

8. Fearless Leader

"All right, time is running and out and we need to get planning. *Valentine's Day moves for no one!*" said Susan, rubbing her hands together.

Amanda brushed the last traces of cookie crumbs from her lips.

"Now, we're glad that Amanda is back," Susan nodded at her, "and that we have the whole team together for a change. But we still need a leader to keep track of everything. So what I propose, what I *suggest*, is that we appoint the most *obvious* person, the *logical* choice…" Susan took a breath. "Which is, of course…"

"**Tim!**" declared Alice.

Tim's cheeks suddenly flushed pink. "Huh?"

"Um, what?" stammered Susan. She had been preparing to nominate *herself*, and this was a complete surprise. "Why *Tim?* I mean, he's not even in middle school yet."

"Exactly," said Alice, nodding. "That's why it should be Tim."

"Do you mind explaining *why?*" asked Becky slowly, leaning forward in her chair.

"Well, it's *really obvious*, isn't it?" said Alice, looking around the table. The confused faces told her it wasn't obvious at all.

"Well, we all know Tim has good ideas, and he's always taking notes," Alice began.

A few nods.

"And he's a very *logical thinker*, which is really important right now. We need clear heads to do this right, and Tim's the best person for that, and I will explain why."

The Valentine's Day Project *Disaster*

Alice took a deep breath and looked at Susan, and then Becky before speaking. "But first, I have to say that I am worried about the two of *you* as well. Cupid's arrow has already taken down Amanda," she gestured towards Amanda, who seemed to be paying attention but still had a slightly dreamy look on her face, like she was thinking about something else.

"Middle school is *dangerous* territory. I mean, you have teenagers there, and we know they're all a bit nuts. They start acting weird, up and down moods and everything. I mean, look at Amanda, she's barely with us, even now!"

Alice sat up straighter, and looked around the table. "Amanda is only a *few months away* from being thirteen, and look at her! Becky and Susan, you're not far behind her. There's no saying when- or if- you might start losing your minds too!"

All the boys nodded. "Yep, Amanda has been acting really weird lately."

"Um, Susan seems OK so far..." said James, squirming in his seat. "But better safe than sorry."

He ignored the sharp glare from Susan.

"But why not you? Why not one of us, then?" asked James.

Alice took a deep breath and paused before speaking. "Well, Tim is *very logical*, and we need that," she began.

Fearless Leader

Several nods.

"He's *well organized* too."

More nods.

"But the *main thing* we need to watch for here, the Achilles Heel sticking out, just waiting to be shot by Cupid's arrow - is *emotion*," she declared.

"We need someone with *practically no emotion*. That way, they can't be trapped by Cupid and mess this project up. Just ask yourself, when was the last time you saw Tim upset about anything?" Alice looked around the table.

Everyone sat quietly in thought.

Tom began "Well, there *was* this time in third grade when he got hit by a baseball…"

Ben elbowed him in the ribs. "Doesn't count," he hissed.

"*Right*, so then Tim is our best choice. Without emotion, he'll be practically *invincible*. Just look at him!" she pointed.

Tim sat there quietly, unsure what to say. The pink that had been in his cheeks before had completely drained away. In fact, he looked a bit pale. "Um, thanks, but I'm not sure that…"

Alice continued, talking over him, "…He's our *cool head*, our *mind of reason*. He's our *Mr. Spock*.

The Valentine's Day Project *Disaster*

Heck, he's the closest thing to a *robot* I have ever met!" finished Alice, crossing her arms.

Everyone was looking at Tim now.

"Um, ah, guys, I'm not so sure about this…" began Tim.

"I vote for Tim!" said James.

"Me too!" said Becky.

"Yes!" said Amanda.

"Tim will be the best, for sure," said Ben.

"I agree!" said Susan.

Tim sank slowly back into his seat as they unanimously voted him to be the leader - to be the *Project Manager*.

After they had finished going around the table and congratulated him, Tim stood up.

"Thanks, *I think*. I see that I really have no choice, anyway. So, with *that* decided, it's time to get to work on this project. As it happens, I *do* have a few ideas that might help, as well…"

Becky pulled out a piece of paper.

Amanda handed her a pencil.

Tim cleared his throat. "Now, let's do a bit of brainstorming. What do you think every Valentine's Dance needs to have?"

Fearless Leader

"Chocolate!"

"Balloons!"

"Streamers!"

"Music!"

"Mirror ball!"

"Black lights. We can use the ones from the Haunted House!"

"Tickets!"

For the next several minutes, Becky scribbled furiously just to keep up with all of the ideas.

"Right! Next, let's go over the notes you took from the meeting with Pete, Chip and Todd. Let's see how that lines up with our ideas so far, and see if we can learn how to improve on what happened last year..." began Tim.

After two hours of solid planning, the group stopped for lunch.

"Great sandwiches, Mrs. Jones!" declared Tim, patting his belly. "Thanks!"

"You're very welcome," she replied. "So, I hear that you're going to be running this dance? And it's for the middle school too - congratulations!"

Tim finished chewing the last bit of the sandwich. He swallowed, took a quick sip of milk, and nodded. "Yeah, thanks. It's kind of how things ended up. But we have a good team."

"Well, good luck, I am sure it'll go well," she said, patting Tim on the shoulder.

"Thanks Mrs. Jones," smiled Tim.

"Right, team - back to work. Let's go over what we have so far," said Tim. "We have a good structure around the plan, and the notes from Pimple Pete were actually quite useful, even if he probably didn't mean for them to be. Let's review what we have so far, before we get into more detail."

"First, we had our brainstorming session to collect lots of ideas. Next, we pulled out some common themes, to group the ideas, like Entertainment, Food and Drink, Decorations and so on. This forms the basis of what we want to do - our *Work Breakdown Structure.*"

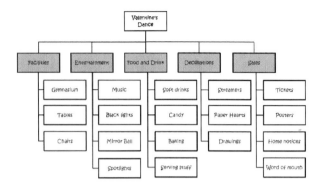

"Next, we took a look at all of these ideas and turned them into groups of *tasks*, based on our *Work Breakdown Structure*, and any more we need to add, like Final Setup. Remember that tasks are actions, so they should have verbs in them. Some tasks need to happen before others, and these are our *dependencies*. So this is what we came up with before lunch."

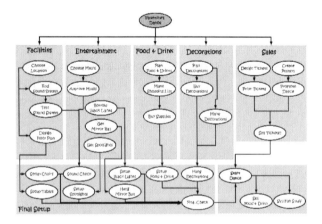

"This project doesn't have a lot of dependencies between the different groups of tasks, but there are a few. This means that we can work on tasks in each of the groups at the same time, which helps when we have a good sized team like ours. Of course, the Final Setup group is dependent on just about everything, where we put everything up and finish getting ready on the day of the dance."

"Now that we know the main things we need to do, and generally in what order, we can put the plan and schedule together. Time is running out, so we need to see how much we can do at the same time, like we did for the Haunted House," continued Tim. "So, we add boxes on each task, so we can write the *task estimates*."

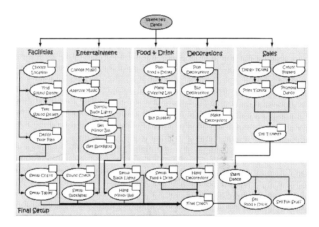

"We don't really know how long some of the things will really take, because we're not sure how much of the truth Pete was telling. But, we can guess, or *estimate*, and add a little extra time to those tasks just in case, as a *contingency*," finished Tim.

Fearless Leader

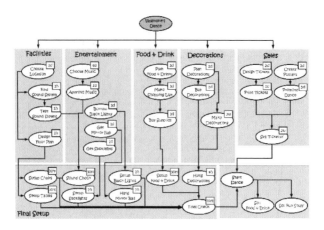

"This isn't as complicated as some of our other projects, although it's still a lot of work. The **Decorations** and **Sales** groups of tasks are almost the same amount of time, just over three weeks, which is about what time we have left after today. The big job in there will probably be making the decorations. We will promote the dance and sell tickets as soon as we have some posters made, and we will just do some of that each day. The other groups of tasks won't take that much time to do. However, there will be a lot to do on the final day, which will be tough, so we will have to ask Ms. Moldiva if we can start some of the setup the day before the dance, or even earlier."

Tim pulled a fresh sheet of paper from the pile and picked up a pencil. "OK, so let's see how we can put this together. We can change things around a little and draw it like this, so we can see it more like a schedule, and we can assign tasks to people," said Tim, scribbling for several minutes.

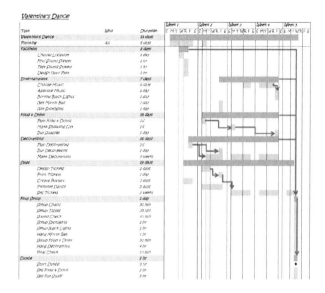

"There, I think that's easier to see what we need to do and when. We can get some of the tasks done earlier, of course, but we should only bring in some of the things like the black lights just before the dance. What do you think?" Tim looked around the table.

Everyone was nodding, even Amanda.

"It looks so simple now that we have it down on paper," Amanda sighed. "I don't know why I was freaking out so much."

Tim grinned. "OK, so next, we need to assign people to each task, and then get moving!"

Fearless Leader

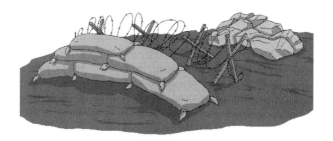

9. No-Man's Land

On Friday at lunch the school cafeteria was serving chili dogs. Amanda, Becky and Susan found a table in the far corner and were just about to start eating, when they noticed a commotion at the far side of the room.

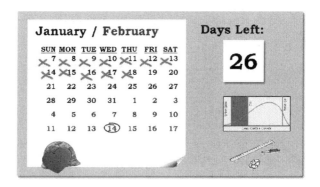

Pimple Pete was shoving his way through the cafeteria, making a beeline toward the girls. Sounds of "Hey! Watch out!" and the splatting sound of chocolate milk cartons hitting the floor followed in his wake.

Amanda calmly bit into her chili dog, and chewed slowly. She watched Pete shove aside the last two smaller boys who separated the girls from Pete's wrath.

He walked up and banged the table, making the plates jump. A splash of chocolate milk escaped from one of the cartons. "*What do you think you're doing?*" he yelled in Amanda's face.

Amanda stared back at him, slowly chewing. Pete was getting even redder in the face. "**What, you won't even answer me? Hah!**"

Amanda finished chewing, swallowed and took a sip of her chocolate milk. The deliberate slowness of her movements made Pete even angrier. "**So, what? You're too good to talk to me, are you, you - you *seventh grader?***"

"**Rude**," said Amanda calmly.

That took Pete by surprise. "**What? Huh?** What are you saying?"

Amanda brushed her hands on her lap, then leaned forward to stare hard at Pete. "It's *rude* to talk with your mouth full of food," she said. "Just like it's *rude* to push people and knock over their lunch. I think, no, *I am sure*, that you owe a number of kids an apology, and new lunches."

"Who do you think you are, ***girl?*** Who are you to talk to me like that? ***After what you've done***," he raised his voice and turned towards the rest of the kids in the cafeteria, who had all stopped moving and were openly staring at this display.

"**After what you've done - *outsourced* our dance to the primary school?**" Pete accused, waggling his finger in Amanda's face.

"**Traitor!**" he yelled. "You're in *big trouble* now, I just came from the principal's office and and..." he looked over his shoulder, "...and there she is now!"

The loud buzz in the room fell to the barest whisper, and then dead silence as Ms. Moldiva made her way slowly across the cafeteria. A clear path melted away before her as children hurried to get out of the way. The click-click-click of her high heels was the only sound in the room as she approached the girls' table. Pete looked smugly at the three girls as he stepped to the side, out of the way of the approaching principal.

Ms. Moldiva stopped just in front of the table. She looked at each of them in turn, and then glanced at Pete, who quickly lost the smug look. "Come vith me, please," she said. "Now."

Amanda suddenly felt hollow as she quickly stood up. Susan and Becky followed, sliding their chairs under the edge of the table. They left their lunch plates where they were.

Ms. Moldiva crooked her finger and said, "Follow me," as she started to walk back across the room. The girls obediently walked around the edge of the table and followed the principal through the hushed crowd. Pete started to follow behind them, his face in full-smug mode, when Ms. Moldiva turned. "No, you - *stay*," she ordered. "I vill talk vith you afterward, young man."

Ms. Moldiva held open the cafeteria door as the three girls filed through. Amanda heard the buzz return, stronger than before, as the cafeteria door pulled itself shut.

The girls fidgeted in their seats in front of Ms. Moldiva's desk. Ms. Moldiva paced back and forth behind her desk before she finally sat down and pulled her chair forward.

"***Is zis true?***" she asked, her stern gaze flicking back and forth between the three girls. "Is zee dance now being organized by children from zee **primary school?**"

"Um, well, kind of, maybe..." began Susan.

"*Maybe?*" said Ms. Moldiva, her pointy white teeth showing as she set her face in a grim smile. "Zere is no 'Maybe'. Zere is Yes, or No. Vich one is it?"

The Valentine's Day Project *Disaster*

Still not quite sure about her saying she's not *a vampire,* thought Becky. *Sometimes she really does look like one.*

Amanda leaned forward. "Both. We are doing the dance, but we have asked for some help."

Ms. Moldiva leaned back in her chair. "Please explain."

Amanda sighed. "Well, we *tried* to get helpers from our school, we really did. We asked over a *hundred people* - and they all said no."

Becky spoke up. "Yeah, nobody wanted to help. They heard about the dance last year, which was apparently a disaster."

Ms. Moldiva leaned further back in her chair, index fingers pressed to her lips. "Yes, I have heard about zat, zee dance last year before I came here."

She rocked her chair back and forth a few times, then suddenly leaned forward, resting her elbows on the desk. "I had thought it was maybe just a rumor. And zee person who organized it last year, zee boy, what was his name?"

"Pimple Pete," blurted Amanda. "I mean, Peter Johansen."

"I see, he was zee one who came to talk to me," Ms. Moldiva said, nodding. "Zee boy in zee cafeteria."

Susan nodded. "Yes, that's him."

"Interesting. He suggested to me zat *he* should organize zee dance this year," mused Ms. Moldiva.

"But now *I don't think so*. I vill have a chat with zis young man. Now, tell me more about zese children from zee primary school who are helping you."

Susan and Amanda exchanged glances, but Becky spoke first. "Ms. Moldiva, do you remember the Haunted House?"

A bright smile appeared on the principal's face. "Yes, I quite liked zat one, especially zee coffin."

"Well," said Becky, pausing to take a deep breath, "it's the same people, except we also have Amanda's little brother Ben helping this time too."

Ms. Moldiva relaxed, leaning back in her chair, gesturing expansively with her hands. "Ah, vell, zat is *good* then! Our plans to have zee older children vorking vith zee younger ones, it takes on a life of its own, yes? If zee dance is as good as zee Haunted House, it vill be vonderful!"

She tidied the small stack of papers in front of her, smiling even wider. "**Zis**, I approve of. You three continue your preparations, vorking vith those primary school children. Let me know if you need anything."

Susan, Becky and Amanda rose from their chairs and walked to the door. They were about to leave the office when Ms. Moldiva called out, "**Vait!**"

Thinking Ms. Moldiva had suddenly changed her mind, Amanda cautiously turned to face the principal. "Yes, M'am?"

"You vill need permission from Mr. Jenkins, zee principal of Wilkins Primary School, so they can come and help you here at lunchtime," she said. "There is a lot of work to be done, and you cannot do it all after school. They vill need permission to come here, through the fence, so I vill write a letter for you. Come pick it up at zee end of zee day."

"Thanks, Ms. Moldiva!" grinned Amanda, then left the principal's office.

As they passed the secretary, they noticed Pimple Pete sitting in a chair in the hallway.

"What are *you* doing here?" asked Amanda.

"I'm here to get *our* school dance back," smirked Pete, but the smug look on his face quickly faded when he realized the girls were actually smiling. *Things might not be going as planned*, he thought.

Becky nodded at Pete. "The principal will see you now."

Pete stood up slowly and walked toward the principal's office.

"Yeah, she said *she wanted to talk to you*," said Susan.

Pete looked over his shoulder at the girls and gulped.

No Man's Land

10. Behind Enemy Lines

"The gym looks a lot bigger when it's empty," observed James. They were inspecting the middle school gymnasium for the next stage of planning.

"I mean, it'll take a *lot* of decorations to fill this place," he said, tucking the school pass deeper into his back pocket. Mr. Jenkins, the primary school principal, was happy for them to help at the middle school, but they had to get a pass from the school office each day that they went over to help.

"Well, maybe we could just decorate *half* of it," suggested Ben, as he looked around the gym.

"No, we want to do this properly," said Tim, frowning at the suggestion. "Besides, Amanda said this needs to be the best Valentine's Day Dance they've had in years."

"Not..." he paused to look at the stage, "...not that that would be very hard to do, from what we hear."

Tim sighed. "Still, we want to do a good job of this, so let's look at the plan again."

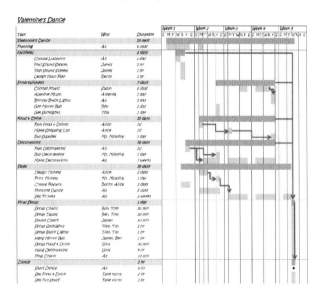

"We have to show *Pimple Pete* we can do it properly," said Becky.

"He is *so annoying*," said Susan.

"He's just a *bully*, plain and simple," declared Amanda.

"So!" said James, rubbing his hands together. "Where do we start?"

The children spent the next thirty minutes walking around the gym, picking good places to hang decorations and measuring distances between beams by counting the steps between them.

Tim consulted the planning sheets on his clipboard and pointed at the stage. "OK, music will be up there on the stage, as well as any prize-giving."

Tim walked over to the side of the gym, along the rows of bleachers. "Kids can sit in the bleachers and around some of the tables, and we can put the tables for drinks and food over here," he flipped over the top page and tucked it behind the clipboard.

"How much are we going to charge again?" he asked Susan.

"Well, Ms. Moldiva said this was supposed to be a bit of a fundraiser as well. So...two dollars to get in, fifty cents for a cup of soft drink or punch, one dollar for a muffin and fifty cents for a cookie,"

Behind Enemy Lines

Susan said, reading a crinkled sheet of paper. "We could also sell other stuff too, like glow sticks, but of course we would need to buy that stuff first."

"Hmmm. That brings us to the *budget*," said Tim. "How much money was in the budget last year?"

Amanda spoke up. "Five hundred dollars."

Ben gave a low whistle. "That's a lot of money. Why do they need to do fundraising if they have money like that?"

Becky shook her head. "It's not that much, not for a dance. Besides, they only made three hundred dollars last year, so they actually *lost* money."

"Oh!" said Ben, the smile fading from his face. "That's not good."

"No, it's not," sighed Amanda. "And that's why she is only letting us have *four hundred dollars* for the dance this year."

"Ouch!" said Tom, "even worse."

"She said that when we have the list of everything we need, we are to bring it to her, with the most important stuff on top. That way," she said, looking around the circle of faces, "if it costs too much money to get all of it, we'll only be able to get the most important stuff."

"*Double* huh," said James. "Sounds like we're doomed already."

The Valentine's Day Project *Disaster*

"No, not necessarily," said Alice. "We just need to be *creative*. Remember we had to do that with the tree house, so we could buy more nails and stuff?"

Everyone nodded.

"Right, so we just need to do the same kind of thing, but probably not with a lemonade stand this time," said Alice.

"We could bake cookies and sell them," suggested Susan.

"Well, maybe we could do some for the dance. Besides, that will cost our moms money to start with, and the school would get the money, which might be OK for a few plates of cookies, but not for hundreds of cookies. There must be a better idea," said Alice.

"Tim, have you finished with the list yet?" she asked, pointing at the clipboard.

"Just about," said Tim, "most of it, anyway."

"So let's look at what we need to get," said Alice, walking over to look at Tim's clipboard.

"OK, let's see," said Alice as she read the list.

Music

Streamers

Balloons

Bows

Behind Enemy Lines

Hearts

Soft Drinks

Punch (Juice, Sprite, Fruit)

Cups

Plates

Muffins

Cookies

Chocolate

Glow Sticks

Prizes

"Hmmm," said Alice. "Some of the stuff we will just have to buy, like soft drinks, things to make the punch, and glow sticks, chocolate and materials for decorations."

Becky pointed at the list. "Some things we can make ourselves, like muffins and cookies, though it would be a lot of work."

"They have the PA system already, we just need someone to plug in some music," suggested James.

Amanda nodded. "Yes, that could work..."

"*But what if nobody comes?*" asked Tom. "That was the problem last year, and we don't even know how many might come this year. If anyone wanted to come, don't you think you would have at least got a *few* volunteers? It might all be a waste, making all of those cookies and decorations if nobody shows up. That sounds like a pretty big *risk*."

"No problem, I could help eat the leftovers," said Ben.

James elbowed him. "Only if you bought them first."

Ben frowned. "Oh, right, of course. *But if they fell on the floor, you couldn't sell them...*"

"*Not going to happen*, we'll be watching you," warned Amanda.

"Hey, just kidding!" said Ben, holding both hands up in the air.

"Uh-huh," said Amanda, unconvinced.

Tim stood quietly watching the others. Finally, he spoke. "I think I may have a solution to both problems."

Tim flipped back the top sheet of paper and smoothed it down on the clipboard. "Actually, make that *three* problems."

Tim counted on his fingers. "**One:** the most important one, is getting people to come. We need people to *actually want to come.* **Two:** we don't want to make or buy too much stuff if only a few people come, or it will be wasted. Besides, we probably won't have enough money for all of the things on our list anyway. Which takes us to **Three:** we need to get people to help by giving us what we need - for *free*."

Behind Enemy Lines

Amanda threw her hands up in the air. "Agh! We tried asking for help already, and it *failed*. *Nobody* wanted to help, that's why you five are here!"

Tim smiled and nodded. "*Correct*. You *asked* people to help, and it didn't work. But we're not going to *ask* people to help. We are going to *convince* them to help, without them even realizing it!"

"How?" began Susan, confused. "I mean how can you, a *Little School* kid, convince *any* of these middle school kids to help?"

"Not," she added hastily, "that I think you're *just* a Little School kid. But you know what I mean."

Tim grinned. "Yeah, well they *would* probably laugh in my face if I asked them to help."

"*However*, what I am thinking about is something that solves all of those problems in one go, and reduces the *risk*. Not only that, it will be so *irresistible* they can't help but help us!" declared Tim, making a note on the clipboard.

"So, what is your big idea then?" asked Becky.

"A *contest*," said Tim. "Actually *two* contests, with prizes."

Tim looked around at his friends. "We haven't eaten any of the Hershey's Kisses you girls paid us yet, right, boys?"

Ben looked at the floor, cheeks pink. "Um, well, I may have opened up *one* of the bags," he mumbled.

Tim shook his head. "So, we have three bags of Kisses, and maybe a handful of loose ones."

Tim turned to look at Amanda. "Your mom makes great cookies, do you think you could get her to bake a few plates for us?"

"Um, yeah, sure, she likes baking. That shouldn't be a problem. But," she said, scratching her head, "I still don't see how any of this helps yet. What kind of contest?"

Tim took a deep breath. "Well, one contest will help with food - so we can have a *baking competition*, with a prize for the best cookies or muffins or whatever."

"The other contest will help with making the gym look nice - we can have a competition for the best Valentine's decoration, and hang them around the gym. We could announce the winners and present the prizes during the dance, so they would have to come," he smiled.

"Great idea," said Susan. "But how do we get them to actually bake cookies and make decorations and stuff?"

"Well," said Tim, taking a couple of steps backward, "we could offer for you girls to give a *kiss* to the entrants in the baking contest."

Behind Enemy Lines

"**Whoa!** *Why, you little brat...*" Amanda raised her fist, shaking it at Tim until Becky put her hand on Amanda's shoulder.

"Um - **Kiss**, like *Hershey's Kiss*, remember Amanda?" Becky winked.

"What? Oh, yeah, right," said Amanda, slowly lowering her arm. "Nice one. Sorry Tim."

"**So**..." continued Tim, "...we'll have an actual prize for each contest, but we award the prizes at the dance. We can even try to get someone to donate some prizes. Then we get people to give us plates of baking for the contest, so we have food to sell. And if they entered baking or a decoration, they will probably want to come and see if they won."

"But if that doesn't work for everyone," said Tim, "the other competition should work for the others. And the best part is that if we can get your principal to agree, *we* won't even have to decorate at all."

"Huh? How would we do that?" said Susan.

"If we can get them to make decorations, put their names on them, *and* put them up in the gym for judging before the dance, we will have the gym almost completely decorated - without lifting a finger!"

"Well, we would have to do a *little bit*, add streamers and balloons and stuff - which are pretty cheap and fast to do," said Becky. "And maybe move a few decorations around if they get clumped together. But it sounds like a good idea."

The Valentine's Day Project *Disaster*

"That's a great idea, Tim!" said Susan. "Where did you get it?"

Tim glanced down at the clipboard, and then looked up, a hint of pink in his cheeks. "Um, well actually it was something I heard Dad talk about the other week."

"When you have a big challenge that you can't do on your own, you can get a lot of people to help a little bit. Sometimes it's for raising money, and sometimes it works for things like this," he said, gesturing at the bleachers.

"He called it *crowdsourcing* or something like that. Everybody helps a little bit, and they each get something small in return. Sometimes there are prize draws too," smiled Tim.

"Cool idea, Tim," said Alice. "Now our biggest problems are taken care of, it will be smooth sailing!"

"*No*, there is a problem - a *big* problem," said Amanda, stepping closer to Tim, glaring down at him.

"*What?* What's the problem?" squeaked Tim.

"If we tell everyone it's us *girls* giving people a *kiss*, that means you must think the *boys* are all going to bring cookies, and the *girls* are all going to do decorations," said Amanda.

"That's just *wrong*. What about *girls* who bring cookies, or *boys* who make decorations?" she crossed her arms over her chest.

"**No**, we need to be fair, and we need to be *equal opportunity kissers*. If it is a girl, one of you boys hands out the kiss. So we won't advertise who is giving kisses, just that we are," said Amanda.

"Sounds reasonable," said Tim, shifting backwards slightly.

"Unless, of course, some girl *doesn't* like chocolate and demands a *real* kiss from our *fearless leader*," Amanda frowned. "Remember, this was *your* idea."

Tim flushed bright pink. "Um, ah, well, it probably won't come to that..."

"Hey, you forgot something," interrupted Alice.

"What was it?" asked Tim.

"You talked about using the Hershey's Kisses, but what about Amanda's mom's cookies? What are they for?" demanded Alice.

"Oh!" said Tim brightening up. "Those are for *us* while we are setting things up. Projects are hungry work, you know!"

II. Battle Plans

"It'll never work," said Pimple Pete as Amanda passed him in the hallway that afternoon. "*I* won't let it."

Amanda stopped and turned on Pete. "What, are you *threatening* me? Ms. Moldiva said it was OK for my friends to help. We have *permission*, so you can't do anything about it!"

Battle Plans

Pete gave a sly smile that emphasized the large pimple on his left cheek. "Hmph. We'll see about that…" and he walked off, whistling.

Amanda scowled and clenched her fists. "Ooooh, *I hate him!*" she hissed and continued walking towards her science class.

The scowl was still on her face when she slid into her desk, dropping her bag loudly on the floor.

"What's the matter, Amanda?" asked Becky.

"I *hate him!*" she said through gritted teeth.

"Who? Oliver?" said Susan, eyebrows raised. "That didn't last long. I mean, just because he told you to spend time on the dance with us instead of with him…"

Amanda interrupted with a wave of her hand. "No, no, Olly's fine, well I think so anyway. It's that *bully* Pete. He just threatened us, saying he wouldn't let the dance work."

"Hmmm," said Becky. "Shouldn't you go tell the principal?"

"And say *what?* She already knows Pete wants to run the dance but she told him no, *twice*. She'll probably just say he's jealous or something and nothing will happen about it."

"Did he say what he would do?" asked Susan. "If you had something specific he said, you might be able to tell her, and she could stop him."

Amanda sighed. "No, just a vague threat."

"Well, maybe he just wants you to worry, and he isn't going to actually *do* anything," suggested Becky.

"Yeah, he may just be playing mind games, trying to mess with your head," agreed Susan.

"Maybe," nodded Amanda. "Maybe. I guess it would be just like him to do something like that."

"Yeah, that's probably it," said Becky. "Don't worry about it."

"But we had better keep an eye on him, just in case," said Susan.

Becky and Amanda nodded.

"So, what did the principal think of our idea?" asked Tim, munching on a cookie.

The eight children had gathered at Amanda's house after school to continue planning.

"Well," said Amanda, frowning. "She said she thought it was an interesting idea, and it would definitely help with the budget."

"But...?" prompted Alice.

Battle Plans

"But," continued Amanda, "she also said that it was going to be very difficult for us to do."

Amanda slowly looked around the table. "She said, *what if nobody brings any food for the contest, and nobody makes decorations?* I mean, if they make food or make decorations, yeah, sure they would be more likely to come to the actual dance. But what if they don't?"

"But they've *got to!*" said Alice. "It's a great idea! *It just makes sense!*"

"Well, of course *we* think it is a great idea, because it helps *us*, and *we* thought of it," said Amanda. "But we need to convince the rest of the school that it's a great idea too."

Ben scratched his head. "OK, so how do we do that? Did Ms. Moldiva have any suggestions about what we could do?"

Amanda sighed. "Yes, well, kind of. She said what we need to do is really simple, but it's also really hard."

"How can it be both simple *and* hard?" asked James.

"Well, we need to convince them to do this stuff - bring cookies, make decorations and actually come to the dance. But right now, we know that almost none of them are interested," said Amanda.

"The *hardest part* is getting them to change their minds, and in order to do that, we need to learn how to *influence* them, and provide some *motivation* for them to do all of those things."

"Might as well give up now then," grumbled Susan. "We got some pretty definite 'no' answers when we talked to them before."

"But wait, what about the kisses and the prizes?" asked Alice. "That's motivation, right?"

"Maybe for a few, but she said it may not be for most of them," Amanda grimaced. "No, we need to do something else. I mean, we can still do those things too, but we need to work on *motivating* them first. Then hopefully we'll have more people interested, and then hopefully they will *want* to do those things."

"Hmmm..." said Tim. "Did she have any tips that would help us? About what motivates people?"

"A very good question," came a voice from the kitchen doorway. "I may be able to help with that."

"Hi Mr. Jones," said Alice.

"Hi Dad," said Amanda, as he walked over to the table and patted her shoulder.

"So, what are you kids working on this time?" he smiled.

"Valentine's Dance," said Tim. "We're running it."

Mr. Jones raised an eyebrow. "My, that's a big project. How did you end up running that?"

Battle Plans

"It's a long story Dad, but we could use some help," said Amanda. "How was your day?"

Her father looked briefly distracted, staring out into the living room. "Oh, fine I guess. Some challenges with a couple of contractors, but nothing we can't handle." He was a project manager for a local construction company and had helped Amanda and the girls learn how to do the Tree House and Haunted House projects.

"Actually, we kind of have the same problem, you and I."

"Really? How could we have the same problem?" asked Amanda. "You do *big* projects."

"Well, from what I overheard, you have a problem with getting other kids in the school to want to participate in something," he said. "Is that right?"

"Yeah, coming to the dance," said Tim. "It sounds like nobody is interested in it *at all*."

"Well, my problem is not *exactly* like that, but I do have some things on the project that need to be done, and right now, I am having trouble getting people to do some of them," he frowned.

"But you can just *tell them* to do it, can't you Dad?" asked Amanda. "You're the boss, right?"

"Well, technically I might be able to do that, but I don't like to do that very often. It's always better to discuss things with the team so they understand what we are trying to accomplish and *why*. That way, everyone gets to contribute; everyone feels like they are part of the team, and when they get assigned a task, they are generally pretty happy about doing it. And they usually work harder because they understand why that particular job is important."

"But Dad, the other kids in the school aren't part of our team. They didn't want to help at all, that's why we had to get help from Alice and the boys," said Amanda.

"*Right*, well that is definitely a different situation, when they are not on your team - but they are *stakeholders*, meaning that if all goes well, they *will* care about the outcome of your project, the dance, because they will want to go."

"Hmmmm..." said Amanda. "They don't care at all right now."

"They just need the proper *motivation*. However, it's important to know that certain types of *motivation* work better for some people than others," he said, looking around the table. "Can I have a piece of paper and a pencil, please?"

Becky slid a blank piece of paper across the table and Amanda handed her dad a pencil.

"Now, there are two main types of motivation, *intrinsic* and *extrinsic*..." he began.

Amanda interrupted him. "Sorry, Dad, can you please use normal words?"

He smiled. "Of course, well let's draw a picture first."

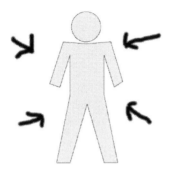

"Extrinsic, or *external motivation* means it is motivation that comes from the *outside*," he said. "That means things like being offered rewards, a bigger salary or allowance, and opportunities to do fun things, stuff like that."

"So, giving people prizes in a contest, or giving them a kiss would be one of those then," said Alice.

Mr. Jones raised an eyebrow and looked questioningly at Amanda. "What's this about kisses...?"

Amanda blushed. "Just *chocolate kisses*, you know, like Hershey's?"

"Hmmm, OK," he said, frowning. "Well, external motivation is the easiest thing for people to try to use, and because it is visible to everyone, some people think that is the *only* way to motivate people."

"However, *external* motivation is not the strongest type of motivation. It may work for a little while, say when you want to get a raise in your salary, but after you get it, pretty soon you think it is normal, and it doesn't motivate you like it did before."

"So, if we gave them a chocolate after they did something, and then they ate it, they would no longer feel any *motivation* to keep doing it?" asked James.

"Kind of like that, yes," said Mr. Jones. "The *expectation* of getting more money or a chocolate may give people an incentive to do something, but it's not long-lasting, and once they get it, the motivation to keep doing things better usually goes away once they have it."

"Or ate it," observed Tom.

"Yes, or ate it," said Mr. Jones, taking a cookie from the plate and taking a bite out of it. "Mmmm. Or if someone offers you a better cookie, you might get distracted and go off to try and get that other cookie."

"So, Dad, what is the *better* type of motivation? The one that works better or lasts longer?" asked Amanda.

Her father flipped the paper over, picked up the pencil and drew a small heart inside another figure.

Battle Plans

"Well, the strongest type of motivation is *intrinsic*, or *internal,* meaning it comes from the inside. When you have *internal* motivation, you are doing whatever it is because you *really, really want to*, and even if someone offers you a better cookie, you are less easily persuaded to change," he said, finishing off the cookie and brushing a crumb from his lips.

"It is the strongest type of motivation, but it is also the hardest for someone else to change in you."

"So...if someone really doesn't want to help or come to the dance, it doesn't matter how many cookies or chocolates we offer them?" asked Tim, making notes.

"Right. They may do or say whatever you want in order to get your cookie, but afterward they'll just keep doing what they want to do," smiled Mr. Jones.

"So what we need to do is figure out how to make people really, really *want* to help us, and then come to the dance," said Tim, frowning. "From the *inside*.

The Valentine's Day Project *Disaster*

But how do we do that? You can't be *inside* someone else's head," said Susan.

"Right, we can't do that. But we *can* think about what may be really important to people, and help them to see that by doing what *you* want, they will also get what *they* want," said Mr. Jones.

Ben slid forward on his chair. "But Dad, how can we possibly know what they want? That's all in their heads, right?"

His father nodded. "Very true, but some very smart people over many, many years have figured out some of the common things that do motivate people on the inside."

Amanda tapped the table with her fingers. "Dad, you are starting to sound like Ms. Moldiva - all confusing. Can you please give us something we can *use?*"

"Sure, honey. I was just about to show you," he said, flipping the paper over and writing:

Acceptance

Recognition

Challenge

Curiosity

Control

Competition

Cooperation

Purpose

Fun

Battle Plans

"There are many different things that can be *internal* motivators, and these are just some of the common ones. Most people want **acceptance** - they want other people to like them, or get **recognition** for what they do," he said.

"Most kids in our school are like that," commented Susan.

Mr. Jones nodded. "Some people like to have a **challenge**, which can be learning a new skill, managing to do something very complex or building something new. But this is because they *want* to do it, not because someone told them to. This often ties strongly into **curiosity** and learning about new things," he said.

"None of those are going to help us much. It'll be a challenge *for us* to get them to help, but I don't think they are curious at all," said Amanda.

Her father smiled. "Well, you never know until you try. You might come up with something that they can be curious about."

"Like a mystery?" said James.

"Yes, like that," said Mr. Jones.

"But what about the other ones in the list?" asked Tim, pointing at the paper. "What about *control?*"

"Ah, well - **control** is a tricky one. Almost everybody wants to have control over what happens to them," he said.

"Like what time we go to bed?" asked Ben. "Can I go to bed half an hour later, Dad?"

His father smiled. "No, you can't. But that's a good example. People like to have control, but they can't always have control over everything they'd like to. Sometimes that makes them behave badly, like trying to boss other people around. People who feel they don't have control of themselves or their environment usually try to control others."

An idea suddenly popped into Amanda's head. "You mean, like a *bully?*"

"Yes, exactly like a bully," he nodded. "Many bullies try to control others because they don't feel they have control over what happens to them, at school or at home. It doesn't excuse what they do, but sometimes it can help explain it, and sometimes understanding it is the first step to begin fixing it."

Amanda nodded. "We have a real bully at school. He keeps trying to take over the dance."

Her father frowned. "Hmmm. Is there some way he could *help* you instead?"

"**No way**, Mr. Jones," Susan shook her head. "He ran the dance last year, and it was terrible. Everybody said he was bossy and hardly anyone came. We don't want him to help - he would probably wreck it."

Battle Plans

"He's already trying to wreck it," muttered Amanda.

"Well, unfortunately you may not be able to change him, but you can try to avoid him. It's hard work getting people to change their behavior, especially bullies. I would suggest just keeping an eye on him for now," he said.

Tim pointed at the paper again. "Why do you have **competition** and **cooperation?** Aren't they opposites?"

Mr. Jones nodded. "Yes, they can be - but not always. If you worked in a team, you would be cooperating, but your team might be competing with another team. So you might be cooperating and competing at the same time. Or maybe there is no competition; you are just part of a team trying to build something new together, which can be very rewarding."

"Makes sense I guess," said Alice.

"But sometimes you may be competing with yourself - like trying to run faster than the last race, that type of thing," said Mr. Jones.

"Another very powerful motivator is having a *sense of* **purpose** - something you strongly believe in. It may be a really big idea, or maybe it's the reason you do a project in the first place. Thousands of people have committed a lifetime of work towards a purpose they really believe in," he said.

Amanda rolled her eyes. "You can be sooo dramatic sometimes, Dad. We just want kids to come to the dance and bake some cookies, not save the world or anything."

"Ah, right," he said, brushing a stray hair flat with his hand. "Well, anyway you get the idea. The last one on the list is **Fun**. Lots of people do things simply because they enjoy them, like watching or playing sports, going for walks, spending time with friends, gardening, making crafts, things like that."

"And playing video games!" said Tom, his hands pressing imaginary buttons in the air.

Mr. Jones chuckled. "Yes, and playing video games. But not until all of your homework is done," he said with a pointed look at Ben.

Ben sighed. "Awww, Dad..."

"But back to **control** for a minute - not all control is bad. There are plenty of good people who get things done because they can influence others to do things, but in a nice way. Good influencers get people to *want* to do things - they don't *tell* them to do it. They're usually good communicators as well, and that's a very important skill to have when you are running a project," he said.

"That's what we want to be, Dad," said Amanda. "We want to be *influencers* and good *communicators*. But how do we do that?"

"Well, to start with, it helps if the people you are talking to *respect* you, or know that you usually have good ideas. That will help to get them listening in the first place," he paused.

Battle Plans

"That'll be hard, Dad, I mean this is *middle school* - and we are only in grade seven. Worse, they are already making fun of us because we have *primary* school kids helping us. Is there anything else we can try?" said Amanda.

"Well, it always helps to be able to tell a good story," he winked.

"We are *not* going to tell kids in our school a bed-time story, Dad. That's silly!" said Amanda.

He grinned. "No, the kind of story that paints a picture of what your vision is, something that will get them excited too. If you can get that idea into their heads, then they will be more likely to want to help you, or do whatever it is you are talking about."

"Sounds *sneaky*," frowned James. "How do they know you aren't telling them to do something bad?"

"Well, sometimes that does happen, and it is very sad when it does. But that's not the case here, is it? It is very important to always tell the truth when you're talking to people because they will very quickly find out if you are not," he shook his head.

"Besides, they will decide for themselves if they like what you are saying. Just because you talk to them doesn't mean you will hypnotize them into doing what you want."

"That's a *great* idea!" said Ben. "We could just hypnotize them, and then they would all bake cookies and make decorations and come to the dance and…"

"It'll never work," interrupted Tim.

"Why not?" demanded Ben. "I've got the hypno-ring I got at a birthday party, it *could* work!"

"That's just a cheap bit of plastic with a swirly sticker," said Tom. "It's not a *real* hypnotist ring."

"But I could learn how to hypnotize *for real*, I mean it would be *fun to do* and…" said Ben.

"Nobody is hypnotizing anybody," said Susan firmly. "Not in *our* school. Things are bad enough already, the last thing we need is half the school running around thinking they're chickens."

"…But it *could* be fun," whispered Ben.

His father smiled. "Sorry, kiddo, like your friends said, it probably wouldn't work. And even if it did, it's not really a good idea. No, you want them to really *want* to do it, all on their own."

Amanda sighed. "Well, we're *doomed* then. I mean, how are we going to convince the whole school about any of this stuff? Like I said, half the school is making fun of us right now."

"Ahhh, well then, I guess you'd better just *give up*," her father said.

Battle Plans

"What? Dad? **No!** You *can't* say that, I mean you are supposed to *help* us. *You promised!*" wailed Amanda, frustrated.

Mr. Jones studied the paper before he looked around the table, a serious expression on his face. "You don't *actually* want me to reveal my biggest *secret*, do you?"

"Yes! Yes! Please, Dad!" said Amanda, exasperated.

"Well, if you insist..." he said, and wrote one more word on the paper.

Advocate

"**Advocate?** Huh? What's that?" asked Alice.

"Let me see how to explain it in middle school terms," mused Mr. Jones. "OK, well who are the kids in your school the other kids look up to?"

Amanda snorted. "Duh, all the *tall* kids, obviously."

Her father shook his head. "No, I mean something different, like who they *respect*."

"Definitely not *us*," muttered Susan.

"Um, the *cool* kids?" suggested Becky.

"Yes, that is one group that might fit," Mr. Jones agreed. "But there may be others as well. Can you think of any kids that other kids ask questions from in class?"

"Um yes, there is Samantha in science class, and Adam in math," said Susan. "They're pretty smart."

"Good, that's another group to consider. Anyone else that the other kids respect, or look up to?" asked Mr. Jones.

"Well, there is Todd, and Chip…" said Becky. "They do sports and stuff, and they tell funny jokes at recess. Lots of kids like hanging around with them."

"OK, it sounds like you are getting the idea. Now, those kids - the cool kids, the smart kids, the kids that other kids like to hang around with - those could be your *advocates*, if you play your cards right," smiled Mr. Jones.

"But what *is* an *advocate?*" asked Susan. "I mean, what do they do?"

Mr. Jones grinned. "Why, they make your jobs a whole lot easier."

The children looked blankly at each other and then back at Mr. Jones.

"What do you mean? How will they do that?" asked Tim.

"Well, if you can convince *them*, the small groups of advocates, that your ideas are good ones, then they'll help convince other kids - *lots of kids* - that it's a good idea too," Mr. Jones smiled.

101

Battle Plans

"Right! Like participating in the baking competition, and making decorations, or even just planning to go to the dance in the first place..." mused Tom.

"So, let me get this straight," said Becky slowly. "We just *talk* to these kids - the cool kids, the smart kids, the ones you call *advocates*, and they just *tell* everyone else to do stuff for us? It sounds too simple. There has to be a trick to it."

"Well, you still have to convince *them*. They really have to buy in to what you are saying, or they won't tell anyone else. You need to be a good influencer and convince them first. So instead of trying to influence the whole school one kid at a time, you can use them to help spread the message faster," Mr. Jones tapped his finger on the little heart inside the figure.

"Because the other kids look up to them, and *respect* them - they will generally respect what they have to say, and more than that, many will want to do what they do. And if your advocates are the first ones to make decorations, or cookies or whatever, then lots of kids will want to do it too."

"You still have to be prepared, and tell a good story. But it can be done, and when it works, it works really well," Mr. Jones said.

"What happens when it *doesn't* work, Dad?" asked Amanda.

"Well, I guess if you really mess it up, then those kids could tell the others to *not* do what you want them to do. That is the power of the advocate - lots of people care about what they think," said Mr. Jones. "For good, or for bad."

"Well, we had definitely better not mess it up then," said Tim. "We need to be prepared, and have the right people talk to them. I mean, the right *person*."

"Who is that? There is no way they are going to listen to any of us, because we are in the little school," said Alice.

"**Susan**," said Becky firmly. "Susan seems to know half the school already and some of them seem to actually listen to her too."

Mr. Jones smiled. "So, you may already have one potential advocate in your midst."

Susan shook her head. "I don't know *everybody*."

"No, but you *do* talk to some of the cool kids, and at least half the smart kids, and we can both talk to Todd…and Chip," said Becky, blushing. "I think they'll listen to you."

"We'll have to put together the *right message*," said Tim, picking up a pencil and pulling a blank sheet of paper off the pile.

"Thanks, Mr. Jones, you've been a great help. If we can get some *advocates* on our side, that will help a lot," said Tim. "Not only will we get a lot of kids coming to the dance, but we will save time and money too!" He pulled out the schedule and made a few adjustments, changing the task owner for decorations to 'School' and adding in the line 'Bring baking'.

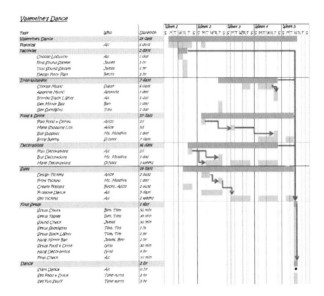

Becky closely examined the sheet of paper. "Looks like a good plan!"

"Yeah, we just need to make it work," said Amanda.

"Have some faith!" said Susan. "I mean, how hard could it be?"

12.Because I Said So

The next day at recess, Susan walked up to a small group of boys standing by the gym door. "Hey Todd, can I speak to you for a minute?"

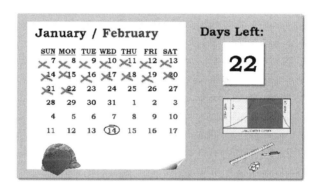

"Um, sure, Susan," he said, and turned to walk away from the group. "Talk to you guys later."

When they were about ten steps away from the group of boys, Susan stopped.

Because I Said So

"Um, so what's up, Susan?" he asked. "You aren't going to ask me to help with your *planning* again, are you? That was pretty horrible."

Susan's cheeks reddened slightly. "Um, no, not really, no…"

"Good," said Todd, turning to look towards the group of boys. "Because I don't ever want to do that again."

"Um, it wasn't *that bad*, I thought…" began Susan, getting redder.

"Yeah, it was pretty bad, all right. So what do you want, anyway?"

"Um, well, I was going to ask you if you could help us…" said Susan.

"Help with what?" interrupted Todd. "Seems to me that you were pretty rude to me last time. Why would *I* want to help *you?*"

Susan's face was now bright red and her hands were starting to shake. "Just *stop it!* I'm sorry about the other day, but we really need your help *right now!*"

Todd shrugged. "That's not the way I see it. You're making me miss out on Stan telling us about his new video game. Why should I help *you?*"

Todd started walking back towards the group of boys.

The Valentine's Day Project *Disaster*

"*Because I said so!*" Susan yelled at his back.

"That only works when you're in *grade three*, and we're not *little kids*, you know - even though *you* hang out with them!" called out Todd over his shoulder, and the group of boys laughed.

Susan stormed off, fighting back tears.

Becky was waiting beside the gym when Susan came stomping around the corner, almost knocking Becky over.

"Whoa!" said Becky. "What happened?"

Susan took a deep breath and gave Becky a brief summary of her conversation with Todd.

"Well, perhaps Todd wasn't the *best* person to start with," said Becky. "I mean, you *were* pretty rude to him last time. You probably should have talked to one of the other cool kids or something."

Susan hung her head. "I'm a *failure*. This dance has been a walking disaster from the beginning and now I just made it *worse!*"

"Well, let's see if we can fix it," said Becky, peeking around the corner.

"There's no point in talking to Todd, I mean he's mad and everything - and besides he would get suspicious if you talked to him too," said Susan.

"No, I wasn't thinking about Todd. He is a bit pig-headed anyway. I'm going to talk to someone a bit more *reasonable*," said Becky, taking another peek around the corner.

She stepped back, brushed her hair with her fingers and straightened her shirt. "How do I look?"

"You look like Becky," muttered Susan. "Who else are you supposed to be?"

"No, I mean do I look OK? My hair is not messy or anything?"

"Um, no, you look fine," shrugged Susan.

"Good! Well, wish me luck, then," said Becky as she walked around the corner and made a bee-line for the group of boys.

Susan waited just out of sight, peeking around the corner. She watched Becky walk up to Chip and talk to him briefly, then the two of them walked over to the picnic table on the far side of the playground. About five long minutes later, Becky waved at Chip and walked back towards Susan, a big smile on her face.

Once Becky was out of sight of the boys, Susan pulled her over to the wall and asked, "So what happened?"

"I think we can count that as one *advocate* on our list," smiled Becky. "Maybe more soon, we'll see."

"How did you do that? Amanda's dad said *I* was the advocate in our group, because I know almost everybody!" Susan shook her head.

"Well, you may *know* a lot of kids, but maybe you don't know *how to talk to them properly*," shrugged Becky.

Susan frowned. "So what did you do? What did you say?"

"Well, I asked to speak to Chip, just like you did with Todd," started Becky.

"And then...?" prompted Susan.

"Well, before he could say anything, I thanked him for being willing to help us before, even though it didn't work out," said Becky. "It also helped that *I* never yelled at him."

"OK, point made, but what did you say?" sighed Susan.

"I was *honest* with him. I told him our idea about getting other kids to help by making decorations and baking cookies and stuff for the contest, to help get them interested in the dance. He said it was an interesting idea, but..." Becky trailed off.

"But *what?* You're killing me!" said Susan, grinding the toe of her shoe into the gravel.

"He said **why?** He asked *why* we were trying so hard, when nobody really wanted to go to the dance anyway?"

"So what did you say?" asked Susan.

"I told him…" Becky paused, "…I told him that I had never been to a Valentine's Dance before, and I really wanted to go."

"So did that convince him then?" asked Susan. "It wouldn't even convince *me*, and *I* am already helping with the dance."

Becky blushed. "Ah, well that was not *quite* everything I said. I told him that I wanted to go to the dance…with **him**."

"**Oh!**" said Susan.

"Yeah!" said Becky, looking at the ground. Her cheeks were a light shade of pink.

"So what did he say?" urged Susan.

"He said he would be *happy* to go to the dance with me," Becky looked up, a bright smile on her face.

"Well, that was lucky," said Susan. "How did you know he would say yes?"

Becky frowned. "I didn't. I mean, I like Chip, but you know, I *thought* he liked me but I wasn't sure. But I was willing to give it a try. That's also why I took him all the way over to the picnic bench. That way, the other boys couldn't overhear if he said no."

"So, you have a *date* for the dance, that's great," scowled Susan. "But what about the *advocate* stuff?"

Becky grinned. "Oh, that's all sorted too. Now that Chip *wants* to go to the dance - *with me* - he wants to make sure it is a *good* dance. So he's going to talk to other kids about it, and he's going to be the first one to bring in some cookies for the contest."

"What about the decorations?" asked Susan. "Did you remember to talk about those?"

Becky looked down at the ground again. "Yeah, we talked about that too."

"So what, is he going to make any decorations, to convince the other kids?" asked Susan.

"**No**," said Becky.

"What?" growled Susan. "He wants to go to the *dance* with you but he won't make any decorations for it?"

"No, *he* isn't going to make any decorations," Becky looked up at Susan, her cheeks bright red. "*We* are. Chip and I are going to the craft room right after school to get started on the first decorations - *together*."

"**Oh!**" was all Susan could say. "**Oh!**"

Because I Said So

After that, things got a bit easier. Becky and Chip went up to the cool kids at lunch and told them how this was going to be a much better dance than last year.

"But you helped run it last year, and it didn't go so well," said John, a tall eighth grader who was on the basketball team.

"True, but it's under different management this year, and the new organizers know a lot more about planning," said Chip, winking at Becky.

"Hmmmm," said John, frowning.

"And last year it was run by boys, and this year there are a lot of *girls* working on it," said Chip. "Girls know a lot more about Valentine's and hearts and stuff, so it *has to be better.* I'm already planning to go."

"Hmmmm," said John, "I don't know...but I trust you, Chip. If you say it's going to be a good dance, then I guess it will be."

Chip breathed a sigh of relief. "Yep, and I will *personally* be helping to make sure that it will be the best dance ever. Now, there are a couple more things that I could use your help on with the other kids..."

Ten minutes later, Becky and Chip were walking back towards the cafeteria. Becky couldn't stop grinning. "I can't believe you convinced them to each bring a plate of baking and make *two* decorations, *and* talk to other kids about it!"

Chip smiled. "I've known most of those kids since first grade. Half of them played on my soccer team for the last couple years - and John too, until he tried out for basketball this year and got too busy. We help each other out; it's as simple as that."

"You sure have nice friends," said Becky.

"We do OK," said Chip. "But now we had better make sure the dance is a success, or they'll never let me hear the end of it!"

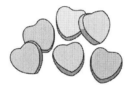

Susan went to speak with some of the smart kids next. Becky thought that would probably be safe, as Susan hadn't yelled at any of them - recently, anyway.

Susan spoke to Adam first, and gave him a short outline of what they were planning for the dance.

"So the dance will be great this year, you should definitely go," said Susan. "It will definitely be way better than last year."

"I wouldn't know, I didn't go," said Adam. "But you do make it sound like fun…"

"*And* we are having a contest for the best baking and decorations, with really cool prizes being awarded at the end of the dance, you should definitely make some," Susan flashed a dazzling smile. "A smart person like you is bound to make the best cookies, or maybe decorations I think - you could almost probably win."

Adam pondered this for a few moments.

"*Two*," he said.

"Um, sorry, what? Are you saying you are going to bring two plates of baking, or make two decorations?" asked Susan.

"Make that two, *and* two," said Adam.

"Two what?" asked Susan, getting frustrated.

"I will help you talk to the other kids, but I want two cookies," said Adam.

"No problem," said Susan. "I can bake you some myself."

"Chocolate chip, please," nodded Adam.

"Is that it?" asked Susan.

"No, I said two - *and two*," Adam shook his head. "I would like *two* cookies…and *two dances*. *With you*," said Adam, raising one eyebrow.

"**Oh!**" said Susan, blushing. "Oh! Ummm, OK, sure, I guess. Are you - *are you asking me out to the dance?*"

Adam studied Susan carefully before responding. "No, I will meet you there. I just want to have two dances, maybe *three* if you are any good…my mom put me in dance lessons last year, you know."

Susan started to roll her eyes but stopped herself just in time. "*Sounds great*, Adam - I can't wait. Now, *who should we talk to first?*"

Because I Said So

I3. Green-Eyed Monster

"*Who* did you say you were going to the dance with?" demanded James, pointing a finger at Becky. She was busy writing down notes as Susan filled everyone in on what had happened with the advocates over the last few days.

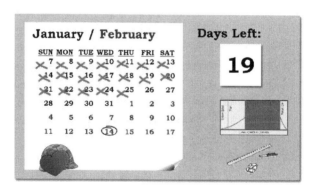

Becky glanced up from the piece of paper she was writing on. "Chip."

117

Green-Eyed Monster

"But-but **why?**" asked James, shaking his head. "I thought he and Todd were pretty clear they didn't want to have anything to do with us after Susan yelled at them. Why would you ask *him?*"

"I only yelled at Todd," corrected Susan.

"Did you just do it to get help with the dance?" persisted James. "I mean, why else would you…?"

Becky placed her pen down on the table and stared pointedly at James. "I **like** him."

"But you like lots of people. You like *me* too, right?" asked James, uncertainly.

"Yeah, sure," Becky waved her hands in the air. "What about it?"

"Um, well, I …" stammered James.

"What, *did you want to go the dance with me or something?*" demanded Becky.

James stared down at the table, cheeks slowly turning red.

"I, oh, um, well, I see," said Becky slowly. "You *did* want to?"

James nodded slowly, staring straight at the table as a small tear ran down the side of his nose. He rubbed his nose with the side of his hand before it could fall onto the table.

"Oh, man, James, *I'm sorry*, I didn't know. I mean, I didn't think we *could* invite anyone from outside the

118

middle school," said Becky. "I read it in the rules from last year."

Tim and Alice exchanged glances across the table. *Here comes trouble…*

"But we're helping you anyway!" protested James. "It wouldn't have mattered, we're going to be there anyway, right?"

Amanda stuck her hand in the air. "Hold up, we might have a problem here."

"What's the problem, Amanda?" asked Susan.

"It just occurred to me that we got permission to *organize* the dance with the help of Alice and the four boys from the primary school, but…" paused Amanda.

"But what?" asked Alice.

"…But we don't know if they are actually allowed to *come* on the dance night!" said Amanda. "What if they are only allowed to do the planning, but not be there to run it? Us three can't possibly do it all by ourselves, especially now that Becky has a *date* with Chip."

"What, like *you* aren't going to be spending time with Oliver?" accused Susan. "That just leaves me to run the whole dance myself. That's not fair!"

"Someone might ask you," suggested Tom. "Who knows, it could happen."

Green-Eyed Monster

Susan fixed Tom with an icy stare. "I'll-have-you-know-someone-has-asked-me!"

"What, for *two dances*, maybe *three* if you are any good at dancing?" scoffed Ben. "That's not a *date*, that's like an appointment with the dentist or something."

"***Who told you that?***" yelled Susan, glaring around the table until her eyes locked on Becky.

Becky swallowed slowly and picked up her pen. "I thought it might be important, you know, like for the lessons learned on how to deal with people. So I wrote it in the project notes. Everyone's allowed to read them."

"I'm surprised that Ben reads anything other than comic books," snarled Susan. "Those are about his speed."

"Hey! I read *graphic novels*," protested Ben.

"Yeah, comics, graphic novels, whatever, same thing," muttered Susan. "The point is that was *private*."

"Not if it's in the project notes," Ben declared, crossing his arms over his chest. "That's an open record."

"Well, *somebody* shouldn't have put it in there in the first place!" said Susan, glaring at Becky again.

Becky just shrugged and drew a flower in the corner of the sheet of paper.

The Valentine's Day Project *Disaster*

"We need to fix this," whispered Tim.

Alice nodded.

"Fix what?" asked Susan, taking a deep breath. "The project notes? It's too late for that."

Tim shook his head and waved his hands in front of him. "No, I mean this - everything. Whether we boys and Alice can come to the dance to run it with you, because..." he paused, "...you three still need help to run it as well, dates or no dates."

Becky opened her mouth to speak but Tim raised his hands higher. "Sure, you can dance some. But we still need you to help. The bigger problem here is that all of you need to stop *arguing* and picking on each other. We've got a lot to do, and we need everyone working together, **so you have got to stop picking each other apart!**"

A stunned silence fell around the table. Susan's mouth had fallen open and James was staring at Tim with his eyebrows raised high. Even Amanda was lost for words. Tim hardly ever raised his voice.

Alice broke the silence. "See? That's why Tim needed to be the leader this time. The rest of you are losing your minds over this silly Valentine's stuff. I tell you, this Cupid thing is like an invisible, evil Robin Hood or something, lurking around just waiting to strike!"

"More like a zombie slowly eating your brains," muttered Tom.

121

"Yeah, whatever, but you get my point. We have to watch out, or it will sneak up and get you. First Amanda, then Becky, we had a close call with Susan, and now James is affected. No one is safe!" declared Alice, glancing at Tim, who nodded back.

"Right! Now, let's hear what my Tim has to say," began Alice, smiling at Tim, then stopped and looked around the table in horror.

"***Agh! No! Not now! Not me too!***" wailed Alice.

Tim raised an eyebrow and frowned. "What's the problem?"

Alice placed her hands on the table and took two deep breaths. "*Nothing…nothing.* Just a poor choice of words, must have been an accident. Yeah, that's what it was," she muttered to herself and shook her head.

Tim lowered his eyebrow and picked up a sheet of paper in front of him. "Right, well, I'm glad that's all over now. Amanda - you need to go to the office first thing on Monday and sort things out so we can all be there to run the dance."

He made a note on the paper, nodded, and then looked around the table. "Now, how many decorations do we have so far?"

I4.Rumor Has It...

"Things are going pretty well," said Amanda as she took a big bite out of her sandwich and placed it back in her lunch box. She finished chewing and wiped her mouth with the side of her hand.

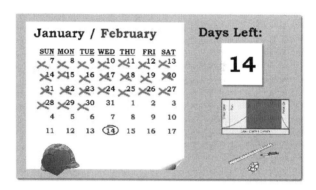

She held up her right fist and raised a finger. "**One:** Ms. Moldiva was happy to grant us an exemption for Alice and the boys to be there for the dance -

seeing as they are helping to organize it. She said it totally makes sense."

Susan nodded. Becky looked down at the table and mumbled "I didn't think…"

Amanda shook her head and raised a second finger. "Doesn't matter now. **Two:** The shopping list is finished and prioritized, and I handed it in to Ms. Moldiva this morning."

"**Three:** The advocate thing seems to be working, thanks Becky and Susan. We already have ten decorations hanging up in the craft room, and I saw a few more being started. Well done - we just need to remind people about the baking. We need some posters done up, and Ms. Moldiva said we could send some information slips home with students."

"I can do that. Chip's pretty good at drawing, we can work on them after school," blushed Becky.

Amanda nodded. "Thanks Becky. Now, **Four:** Susan, how's the music selection coming along?"

Susan grinned. "Great!"

"So, how many songs have you picked?" asked Amanda.

Susan hesitated. "Umm, well, I don't know."

Becky turned to look directly at Susan. "What do you mean, you don't know? Did you pick the music or not?"

124

Susan shrugged. "Not exactly, I *delegated* that to James."

"You're letting a *boy* pick the music for a Valentine's dance?" Amanda shook her head. "I hope you know what you're doing…"

Susan reddened. "I thought that was supposed to be a good leadership thing, you know, *delegating tasks* and stuff."

"Sure, yes, well it is, but the music part is kind of *important*, if we want people to actually dance and stuff," sighed Amanda. "But you are *accountable* for the music, you can't just give the job away. So you have to make sure James does a good job."

Susan dropped her hands onto the picnic table. "So you mean it will be *my fault* if the music is bad, even though I didn't pick it?"

Becky nodded. "Yup."

"But that isn't *fair!*" whined Susan. "If James picks bad music, why would it be *my fault?*"

"Because Tim assigned the job to *you*," shrugged Amanda. "You need to deliver good music. Everyone is counting on it."

"But…but…" said Susan. "OK, well, if everyone will blame me if the music is bad, then I'd better do it *myself!*"

"Nope, it's too late for that," said Amanda.

"But *why?* I'll just take the job back from James, it's *easy!*" declared Susan.

"You have to give James a chance," said Becky. "He's upset enough about me going to the dance with Chip, if you take this away from him, he might just quit and not help us at all."

"Besides, that's not what good leaders do," said Amanda. "Dad said so. When you give someone a job to do, you don't take it away from them, except as a last resort if they totally mess up or what they are doing might hurt someone. You have to let them *try* to do a good job, and learn how to do it better next time. Besides, we already know us three girls aren't enough to get it all done, we need the boys and Alice. So they need to have jobs too."

Susan crossed her arms and plonked her forehead down on the table. "So what do I DO?" she wailed.

Amanda patted her on the back. "Well, you can let James sort through lots of music, that's the tough part anyway. You may want to tell him what kinds of music to look for, to make it easier."

"And then...?" asked Susan, peeking up at Amanda from under her hair.

"Then...then you have James bring the music to you for approval," said Amanda. "That way, James gets most of the hard work done, and you can do some *quality control* on the music - you know, choose not to have some songs he suggests, or ask James to look for a few more if there aren't enough of one particular kind."

Susan raised her head and sat up straight. "I guess that makes sense. It won't be that bad."

"No, it should be OK, but..." paused Becky.

"But WHAT?" asked Susan.

"...But absolutely *no yelling at James*," finished Becky. "You need to keep him motivated on the music selection, and yelling at him won't help."

"Yelling? When do I yell at James? Of course, he's my *little brother*, you *have* to yell sometimes, right? Like when he messes up or annoys me or..." Susan quickly glanced at the two girls.

Amanda and Becky exchanged glances, and then blurted out at the same time "NO YELLING!"

"What? But it's not like I yell A LOT or anything..."

"No. Yelling. Period," said Becky.

"Not until the dance is over anyway," said Amanda.

"Zero. Zip. Nada," Becky shook her head.

Susan took a deep breath and let it out in a gush of air. "Somehow I think the *music* part of this is going to be the easiest bit. But I'll *try* not to yell at James until after the dance."

Amanda shook her head. "You'll have to do better than that. As a matter of fact, no yelling at

ANYBODY for the next while. Look what happened with Todd!"

Susan threw up her hands. "OK, OK, I get the message. *No yelling*. Just a smile-and-be-nice Susan. But it won't be easy."

Becky grinned. "The important things rarely are."

"Did you hear?" whispered the boy next to Becky in math class.

"Hear what, Kevin?" Becky whispered back.

"There won't be any more decorations for the dance," whispered Kevin.

"What? Why not?" hissed Becky, trying not to attract the teacher's attention.

"Something about the arts teacher being mad that all of her paper and glue is being used up, so there's not enough left for her classes," he nodded. "It's game over."

"But...but..." whispered Becky, then stopped as the teacher frowned in her direction.

"Talk to you in the hallway after class," he said, nodding at the door.

Becky was the first to leave the classroom when the bell rang. She waited for Kevin to come out, then grabbed him by the arm and pulled him over to one of the lockers. "So, what's up with this stuff about there being no more paper and glue?"

Kevin adjusted his shirt before he spoke. "It's just what I *heard*. You know, school budgets are tight this year, and there is only so much glue and paper to go around - and paint, and stuff. They can't waste it on *extra* things like decorations for a dance. *Education* is more important."

"Oh, and the baking competition is off too, because lots of people have peanut and wheat and sugar allergies and stuff," added Kevin. "That's what they're saying, anyway.

"*Who* is saying all of this?" demanded Becky.

Kevin shrugged. "*Everybody*, the whole school is saying it. So it must be true."

"So how come I'm only finding this out now?" said Becky through gritted teeth.

Kevin shifted uncomfortably. "Um, well, people didn't want to *upset you*, what with you and the other girls working so hard to try to make this dance thing happen…"

"So, *not telling us* was supposed to make us feel better?" scowled Becky. "So *now* what are we supposed to do?"

"Hey, I don't know, OK?" said Kevin, backing up along the row of lockers. "I only told you because I like you. And…"

"And what?" said Becky, trying to keep her voice down.

"Ah, well, it's nothing really, I just thought…" stammered Kevin.

"You thought *what?*" demanded Becky, her voice rising.

"I…well…I thought that maybe you might want to go with the dance with me," mumbled Kevin.

"Sorry, I'm already going with someone," Becky shook her head.

"That's not what I heard," said Kevin.

"***What did you hear, Kevin?***" squealed Becky.

"Um…well, it's just that everyone's saying that Chip really wanted to go with *Caitlyn*, but you surprised him by asking him first, so he was kind of stuck and had to say *yes*…" said Kevin, face turning bright red.

Becky slumped against the nearest locker and grabbed the padlock to hold herself up. "What? Really?"

"...So, I thought that if *he* really wants to go with *her*, then *you* might want to go with...*me?*" finished Kevin.

Becky's head was swimming. "*Chip...Caitlyn?* He never said anything, he seemed happy to...I mean, we did two decorations and everything...but you say...he...her...really?"

Kevin looked at Becky hopefully. "So...do you want to?"

"Huh, what?" asked Becky, feeling dizzy. "What did you say?

"I said, did you want to go to the dance with me?" asked Kevin. "What do you say?"

Becky's vision was swimming. "Not now, Kevin, *leave me alone.* I need to think - and talk to Susan and Amanda - right now!"

"But...but...I was just trying to *help you* and..." stammered Kevin as Becky stormed down the hallway.

"It's not like *anyone else* was going to tell you! I only told you because I *like* you and...aw, jeez..." his voice fell to a whisper in the empty hallway.

"We've got a problem," said Becky when she got into social studies class.

131

"Yeah, sorry to hear about Chip," said Susan.

"What, you too?" asked Becky. "Who else in the school didn't know, besides me?"

"It's the decorations and baking thing that really worries me," said Amanda.

Susan smacked Amanda on the arm. "Hey! Think about *Becky* for a minute. The other stuff can wait."

"Ahem! Your *conversation* can wait until after school," said Mr. Anderson, their social studies teacher. "Social studies does *not* mean being social in class."

Susan and Amanda exchanged smirks and opened up their books. Becky opened up her textbook but she couldn't focus on the words. Her mind was somewhere else.

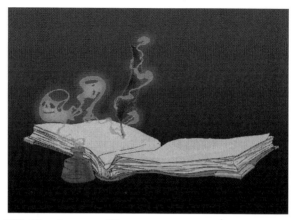

15.Poison Pen

A surprise assembly was called the next morning. As the students slowly shuffled towards the gymnasium, Amanda whispered to Becky. "Why do we have assembly today? It isn't supposed to be until next Friday."

Becky shrugged as she passed through the doorway. Inside, the gymnasium was buzzing with speculation about this unexpected event.

133

Poison Pen

"I hear that there's a rock star in town, maybe they're coming to the school," said a boy on Becky's left.

"Naw, I heard it's an astronaut, bringing moon rocks and everything," said the girl beside him.

"Maybe that dentist is back, to give everyone tickets to the theme park?" suggested another boy hopefully.

Becky just shook her head. Wherever you turned, someone had 'heard' a different story about what was happening. *They couldn't all be right, of course, but which one was true?…And who is the "they" in "they said"?*

Becky sat on the floor and looked around the gymnasium. The last few classes had entered the gym and were finding a space on the floor. The eighth graders had come in first and claimed the bleachers, as usual. Becky noticed Chip give her a small wave, but she decided to ignore him. *He'd rather go with Caitlyn anyway*, she thought.

The lights in the back of the room dimmed as the principal walked up onto the stage. Usually she was smiling when she addressed the students, but something was wrong today. As she walked up the steps, there was no flash of white. Her lips were pressed together so firmly they barely showed at all.

As Ms. Moldiva reached the podium, the room fell silent. She tapped the microphone to confirm it was on. The squeal that echoed around the room was like fingernails on a chalkboard, making Amanda's skin crawl.

Ms. Moldiva swept her gaze back and forth across the room, as if she was looking for someone. After nearly a minute of uncomfortable silence, in which it seemed like she must have made eye contact with every single person in the room, she gave a small cough.

She paused for a moment, then forced a small smile onto her face. It wasn't much of a smile, and all Amanda could see from the twelfth row was the tips of the principal's pointy canines. Amanda shivered, thinking back to the first time they had met Ms. Moldiva.

"I vanted to have a vord with you all today," Ms. Moldiva began. "One vord, but it is very important."

High above and behind the principal, a single word appeared on the screen.

Rumor

She looked back over her shoulder to confirm that it was there for everyone to see. "Zis word is a terrible one. It wrecks so many things, so many people, so many relationships."

She looked out over the room. "How many of you know what a rumor is?"

About half the students raised their hands.

Poison Pen

"I see. Vell, did you also know zat a rumor is like a virus?"

A low buzz crept across the room as students spoke to each other in hushed tones.

"What does she mean, a rumor is a virus? Like a cold or something? Can you catch a rumor?" whispered Susan, frowning.

The principal tapped the microphone again and the room fell silent. "Yes, a rumor acts like zee virus, yes? Maybe not exactly like zee cold or zee flu. It is more like a computer virus for people. But it is most dangerous, because it changes *behavior*."

Even louder buzzing filled the room, and it took two taps of the microphone to call for quiet.

"Yes, rumors are like a virus to zee brain. You hear zee rumor, and if you believe it, you *think* it, and spread zee message to everyone around you. Pretty soon, everyone is *infected*," said Ms. Moldiva, tapping her long fingernails on the side of the podium. She gestured towards the side of the stage, and a short, plump woman dressed in white got up from her chair and began walking towards the steps, carrying a red and white plastic case.

"It vould appear zat vee have a full-scale epidemic of rumors in zis school, and vee need to eliminate them, rig*ht now*. You all need to be immunized against these rumors."

Susan craned her neck to try and see the short woman. *Was that the nurse? What was she carrying?*

As the woman in white neared the podium, she slowed down and stopped just to the right of it. She held the plastic box behind her with both hands and waited patiently as the principal spoke.

"A rumor is a trick message, yes? Zee information sounds reasonable, but is not correct. Someone," she briefly scanned the room again before continuing, "someone or some persons in zis room have been starting zee rumors. Zee rest of you have been spreading them."

So that's what Dad meant when he said that advocates can help spread messages - for good or bad, thought Amanda and shuddered. *Pretty dangerous stuff.*

Ms. Moldiva gave a small cough. "Yes, a rumor is bad information, but zee other term for zis is..." she paused, then raised her voice for emphasis. "**LIES**. Zese rumors are **lies**. And zis - zis, **I do not tolerate**. Not **now**, not **ever**. Not in **my** school."

"And so..." Ms. Moldiva gestured for the woman in white to come closer, "...and so, Mrs. Smith is here to help all of you. While I would like to be able to give all of you a big jab with a needle to protect you from rumors, there is no such vaccine. Instead, vee have zis."

137

Poison Pen

Mrs. Smith walked up to the podium as Ms. Moldiva stepped aside. Mrs. Smith placed the plastic box on the podium and unclipped the sides of the case with a loud **snick**. She opened the lid, removed several objects, and then spoke into the microphone.

"I am Mrs. Smith, the fine arts teacher and part-time school nurse. I am very sad to hear that there are a number of rumors going around, and I am going to stop several of them right now. **One:** that there will be no more decorations because we have run out of paper, glue and paint," she said, holding up several sheets of paper and a glue stick in one hand. The other hand held a tube of paint and several brushes.

"This is definitely **not true**. Every year we plan for events like this, and many other creative projects. We have plenty of materials. In fact," she said, staring at the students, "we have a *surplus* of materials, and I expect *each* of you to make a decoration for the dance. I think it's a fantastic idea, and a wonderful opportunity for artistic expression and creativity. I'm really looking forward to seeing your work on display throughout the gym on the night of the dance, and I would be happy to be a judge for the contest."

"**Two:** someone is spreading a rumor that there will be no baking for the dance because of food allergies. This is also untrue; however we *do* request that none of the baking contain peanuts, as some students have a severe allergic reaction to being near anything containing peanut products.

And while some students may have a gluten intolerance, that is easily solved by putting labels on your baking when you bring it in."

She glanced at the students in the bleachers and smiled. "Now, as for some people being allergic to *sugar* - well, that is technically possible, but it's no reason not to have baking at the dance. Some of you could bring in sugar-free baking and label it. So feel free to bake all you want, and I look forward to buying some of your treats."

Mrs. Smith put the items back into the plastic case and closed the clamps with another **snick**. Then she nodded to Ms. Moldiva and walked back off the stage towards her seat.

Ms. Moldiva walked back to the podium. "As you see, both of zese rumors were false. I believe also that zere are other rumors going around zee school, and I must insist zat zey stop *right now*. If you are not sure about something you have heard, come ask myself or a teacher. As for zee rest, be careful listening to vot you hear, and always be honest."

She scanned the room for a few seconds, and frowned. "Always be honest, because zee lies, they catch up with you, yes? And when I find out who has been *poisoning* my school with zese lies and rumors, vell, I assure you that zee punishment will be severe. *Most* severe."

The principal began to turn away from the podium, paused, and then turned back to the microphone.

"Oh, yes, one more thing. I look forward to seeing you at zee dance - *all* of you. We have some very hard-working children trying to put on a most excellent dance for you, despite these attempts at *sabotage*. I expect you to support them, and to support your school. But most of all, to have fun, yes?"

With that, the principal walked off the stage and the lights came back on. The room swiftly went from a buzz to a roar as hundreds of children began to try and figure out who had started the rumors. Nearly every student was engaged in conversation.

All but one, who stood silently in the shadow of a large pillar. The student slowly shrunk back further into the shadows, until only a large, pimply nose could be seen.

16. One Little Kiss

"Well, that's a relief," said Becky. "I just spoke to Chip, and the whole Caitlyn thing was just a rumor, like the decorations and baking."

"Yeah, someone is trying really hard to wreck our dance," said Amanda, frowning. "And I think I know who it may be…"

"Nah, leave him be. If Pete tries anything else, he's sure to get caught. Besides, everyone in the school is watching out for rumors, so they won't work next time. Anything else would have to be more direct, and I don't think he'd dare do anything now, not with the school on high alert for *dance sabotage*," said Susan.

"Yeah, I suppose so," said Amanda.

"Let's just focus on finishing this project, so the dance can happen without any *more* problems," said Becky. "Besides, today's the first day for ticket sales!"

"That's right!" smiled Amanda. "Oliver said he'd be the first in line. I can't wait!"

"How is Oliver anyway?" asked Susan. "You haven't said much since he told you that you had to focus on the dance."

Amanda frowned. "Yeah, well, he's been taking this whole responsibility thing seriously, and I'm sure he doesn't want to be a distraction."

"Have you spoken to him since then?" asked Becky.

"Um, well, no," said Amanda.

"Not once, even in the hallway between classes?" asked Susan, eyebrows raised.

"Um, no, like I said, he was pretty definite about how important this was for the school..." mumbled Amanda.

"Huh. If it was me, I would still *talk* to him at least a few times a week. Like Alice said, *anything* could happen with Cupid hanging around," Becky said, shaking her head firmly.

"It'll be fine, you'll see," said Amanda, with more confidence than she felt.

Ticket sales opened halfway through lunchtime, with three tables setup in the hallway outside the school gym.

The whole project team was there to help in case there were lots of customers, and they weren't disappointed. They had the bags of Hershey's Kisses sitting on the floor in case someone decided to bring in any baking early, or wanted to hand in decorations.

As he had promised, Oliver was waiting at the front of the line behind the rope. There were around fifty kids in line behind him. "You sell him our tickets," Amanda said to Becky. "It wouldn't feel right if I sold Oliver my own ticket."

One Little Kiss

"Sure, Amanda, no problem," said Becky. "You can sell Chip our tickets, same reason."

Amanda nodded, then walked around the table to remove the rope. "Hi Olly, I missed you."

"Hi Amanda, I missed you too," he smiled, then paused. "Aren't you supposed to be behind the table?"

"Huh? Oh yeah, right, selling *tickets!*" she sang out, springing lightly back to the table, and then took a seat.

Oliver walked up to Amanda, money in hand.

"I'll get your tickets," said Becky, nodding at Amanda. "Two, right? That'll be four dollars."

A frown flashed across Oliver's face, but was quickly replaced with his normal smile. He accepted the two tickets from Becky and walked away from the table.

"Bye, Olly!" called out Amanda, a big smile on her face.

Oliver looked over his shoulder. "Oh, yeah, thanks Amanda, see you soon."

Oliver was nearing the corner of the hallway when a slim blonde girl ran up to Oliver. She plucked one of the tickets from his hand and gave him a quick kiss on the cheek. "Thanks Olly!" she said, and then ran back down the hallway, out of sight. Oliver followed more slowly.

The Valentine's Day Project *Disaster*

Amanda's face rapidly changed through a range of colors. "***What?*** What was that? What did he ***do? Why did she take my ticket?***"

She turned on Becky. "Why did he do that? Why did you sell him those tickets, if he wasn't going to keep one for me?"

Becky was equally stunned, but quickly recovered. "Hey, don't blame *me*, I just work here. Besides, *you* asked me to sell him the tickets. How did I know what he was going to do with them?"

Amanda slumped back in her chair, not noticing the student standing in front of her, waving some money to try to get her attention.

Finally, she grabbed the money and handed the student two tickets without looking at them. "I mean, how could he do that? He was all smiles and everything!"

"Maybe Alice was right. She *did* warn you what could happen," said Susan.

"That's not helping," said Becky. "Can't you see that Amanda is upset?"

"Yeah, I see that, but in the meantime, we have nearly a *hundred kids* who want to buy tickets, and the line is getting even longer!" Susan shook her head, using both hands to take money and hand out tickets to two students at once. "We need some help here!"

One Little Kiss

Lunchtime passed quickly, and soon they had to pack up the ticket sales. Becky kept hoping to see Chip, but he never showed up. "He might still be mad at me for ignoring him," said Becky. "I hope he gets over it."

"Well, at least he wasn't here buying tickets for *someone else*," scowled Amanda.

"Yeah, well, there must be another explanation," said Susan.

"Oh I don't know, it seemed pretty obvious to me," said Amanda. "Like he couldn't even wait to do it out of sight, he had to let me *see* him give that girl my ticket!"

"Um, it kind of looked like she took it from him. I'm not sure he actually *gave* it to her," said Becky.

"Whose side are you on?" sputtered Amanda. "I mean, she's got my ticket, Oliver gave it to her, they let me see it all happen, the message seems pretty clear to me."

"So what's the message?" asked James.

"Ugh! Boys! Like you would even understand," sighed Amanda. "Oliver bought *two* tickets, one for him, one for me. He gave *my ticket* to *another girl*, right in front of me. He's telling me he doesn't want

146

to go to the dance with me, he wants to go with *her*. Isn't it obvious? He just didn't say it out loud, but actions speak louder than words."

"There might be something else going on," said Tim, rubbing his chin.

"Well, Alice is the so-called expert," said Tom. "What do you think?"

Alice shifted her weight from foot to foot and paused before answering. "Well, I'm no *expert*, but it did look like he kind of *dumped* you."

"Aghhh!!" yelled Amanda. "Aghhh!"

"I hate to say this, you being my big sister and all, but I hope all of you are wrong," said Ben. "You might have misinterpreted it. Why don't you ask Oliver?"

Amanda's look shot daggers. "How am I supposed to do that, seeing as he *dumped* me? In public even? Without even saying *anything*, he said *everything*. There's nothing left to say."

"So he wanted me to stay away from him until the dance? That's not going to be a problem - *not a problem at all*."

One Little Kiss

17. Face the Music

The next week went by in a blur. Tickets were selling fast every day at lunchtime, people were registering their decorations for the contest, and the baking had started to arrive. It looked like most of the school would be coming to the dance.

Storing the decorations wasn't a problem, as the students hung them up in the gym after they were registered. The gym was being kept off-limits for

149

ball games for the week before the dance, so the decorations wouldn't get wrecked.

The principal had offered one of the locked closets for storing the baking, but it was starting to fill up. With two days left to go until the dance, they were probably going to need another closet.

Becky had been relieved when Chip bought tickets for the dance. In fact, he bought several extras, "For some of the boys that couldn't make it themselves, because they were in lunchtime detention." Becky was just glad that she didn't see him handling tickets to some cute girl. *Poor Amanda.*

Conspicuous by his absence was Pimple Pete. Apparently he was still at school, but he seemed to be avoiding the dance organizers.

Good riddance, thought Amanda as she handed out tickets to a freckly red-head. *I'm just glad he's not causing any trouble or trying to intimidate us by lurking around.*

"Four hundred and fifty-seven," said Alice, as she closed her notebook. "Pretty good so far, I think that must be the most tickets the school has ever sold - and we still have two days to go!"

"How are we doing on the decorations?" asked Susan.

Alice opened the notebook and flipped through the pages. "One hundred and eighty-nine registered, which is fantastic. The school might run out of glue and paper after all," she winked at Susan.

"Bah, they said not to worry about that. Besides, the dance is already going to make money, and that's not even counting the bake sales!" grinned Susan. "They can buy some more glue and paint if they need to."

"Remember to bring in your black lights, the ones we used on the Haunted House," said James.

"Right, and Ms. Moldiva said the school had a few that we could use for the dance too," said Amanda. "They already have colored spotlights from other dances, so we won't need to buy any of those. They also have a mirror ball, and the custodian will hang up the lights and mirror ball on the day."

Tim picked up the clipboard from the table and flipped through several sheets of paper. "Well, things seem to be going well, but we've said that before."

James groaned. "Don't be so negative."

Tim shook his head. "No, just being realistic. Every one of our projects has had some surprises, and this is the first one we've had that someone is actively trying to wreck."

Tim looked at Alice. "Other than your dog, I mean. But you could hardly blame him for wrecking the haunted house the first time. He's just a dog after all."

Face the Music

"If Pete was a dog, he'd be a mongrel," said Amanda.

"That's not a breed," said Alice. "Did you mean bulldog, or pit bull?"

"Nah, mongrel. He's just *mean*. It doesn't matter what kind of dog breed he would be," said Amanda. "An ugly one, maybe."

"I like cats," said Becky. "They don't tend to bite, and they're not as stinky and smelly as dogs."

Tim smoothed down the papers on his clipboard. "Well, on that note, we need to get back to our school. We don't want to get detention for being late, how would it look if we weren't able to help, so close to the dance?"

"So how's the music selection coming?" asked Amanda as the girls walked home from school together.

"What? Oh, I have to check with James," said Susan.

Amanda raised an eyebrow. "Did you do what we said? Have you looked at the music list?"

"Oh, yeah sure, a couple times, and listened to samples as well. James is doing a pretty good job, actually, but I did ask him to find a couple more songs, just in case. And I asked him to find some slow dance music. Do you know what he thought that meant?" asked Susan.

"No, please tell me," said Amanda.

"He thought you just took a song and played it at half-speed, you know, like those DJ's do when they do special effects with songs." grinned Susan.

"No way, really?" Amanda shook her head. "We warned you about boys picking Valentine's music. I hope you fixed that."

"Yeah, you could say that," said Susan. "Mom had to play him some examples. After he stopped pretending that he was throwing up, he said he'd do it."

"So the rest of the music is good?" asked Amanda.

"Yeah, all good, popular stuff most kids like, should be fine," nodded Susan. "I'll check with James tonight to see how the slow dance music is going."

"Well, the dance is in two days, so you had better get it sorted," said Amanda. "We're counting on you!"

Susan chuckled. "Don't worry, I've got it under control!"

Face the Music

"What do you mean, you couldn't find any slow dance music?" demanded Susan as they set the table for dinner. "You *promised* to find some!"

"Well, sure, there's lots of *old* stuff, like from dead people, or stuff that might make you fall asleep, but I don't think that's what we want," said James. "I think we want something, you know - *modern*. And not *boring*."

"So, have you been actually *looking?*" asked Susan, exasperated. "Or have you just been playing games on the computer? If you have, I'll tell Mom and Dad, you know gaming is only allowed on weekends."

James shook his head firmly. "No games. And yes, I *have* been looking. They just don't seem to make slow dance music for twelve year olds. I had Mom listen to some of the more modern ones, and she said *no way*, not appropriate for kids."

Susan placed the last fork on the table and rested her hands on her hips. "So what are we going to do?"

"Just leave it to me, sis. I have a *plan*," nodded James. "You just have to *trust me*."

Susan shuddered.

The Valentine's Day Project *Disaster*

"What's the matter with you?" Becky asked when Susan shuffled into English class. "You look like you've been rolled over by a truck."

"Maybe that would've been better," sighed Susan, dropping her school bag beside the desk. "Didn't sleep much."

"Why not?" asked Becky.

"Music," grunted Susan.

"What, were the neighbors playing it loud again last night? I didn't hear it," said Becky.

"No, James," grunted Susan.

"James played music? Wouldn't your parents have noticed and told him to stop?" asked Becky, confused.

"Dance music. No slow stuff. James has plan," sighed Susan. The extra syllables seemed to make her even more tired.

"Can you please top talking in grunts? How about, oh, I don't know, *full sentences* or something, so that you actually make sense?" said Becky.

Just then, Amanda walked in and slid into the seat on the other side of Becky. "What's up?"

"Miss Sunshine here is barely speaking. Says she's been up all night," said Becky.

"What's the matter, Susan?" asked Amanda.

Face the Music

Susan squeezed her eyes shut tight, then yawned. She took a deep breath. "There's no slow dance music for kids our age. Nothing that isn't ancient. All the modern stuff has been vetoed by Mom. So instead, James has a *plan*. He says I have to *trust him*, but he won't tell me what the plan is," said Susan, then yawned twice. "Been worried about it all night, hardly slept a wink. James was up until late doing something on the computer, but he had the door locked."

Becky smiled uncertainly. "Well, everything else seems to be on track - all of the food, decorations, drinks, and the gym is ready to go. The teachers will be judging the decorations and the baking just before the dance. The tickets have pretty much sold out now at five hundred and thirty, unless we print some more. Ms Moldiva has even decided to buy more of the stuff from our list like the glow sticks and stuff, so I guess it's just the music left."

"Exactly," groaned Susan. "Just the most important part. The difference between a *dance* and a long boring evening of uncomfortable conversations. Now who would pay for that? What if they asked for refunds?"

Amanda hadn't considered that. "Hey Becky, did we print 'no refunds' on the tickets?"

Becky looked slightly ill. "Um, no, not that I can remember. But they wouldn't do that, would they?"

"What about Plan B?" asked Amanda.

The Valentine's Day Project *Disaster*

"I didn't know we had a Plan B," said Susan. "What's that?"

"If all else fails, we can sing for the slow dances," suggested Amanda.

"Who - us? Not unless you want to hand out double refunds, no thanks. I'm not that great of a singer," sighed Becky. "The dog howls and everything."

"Maybe he was just trying to sing along?" Susan winked.

"Not with his paws pressed over his ears, he wasn't," Becky shook her head. "I tried it a few times, and he did the same thing each time."

Amanda snorted, then began to laugh. "Sorry Becky, that's hilarious."

Becky's face began turning red. "It's not funny."

Susan burst out into giggles, then wiped a tear from her eye. "Yes - it is, it really is."

"No, it's - began Becky, then smiled despite herself. "OK, maybe it is a *bit* funny."

"Funny - you are so good at speeches and stuff. Glad we didn't have to *sing* about our last project. Howoooooooo!" howled Amanda, head pointing to the sky.

"Stop it!" said Becky, trying not to laugh. "Stop it!"

"That's what the dog was saying!" laughed Susan, unable to hold back anymore.

Face the Music

"I give up!" smiled Becky, then burst into laughter.

It took a couple minutes for Amanda to compose herself. "OK, point made. No *singing* for the dance. We'll just have to hope that James comes up with something that works. It's not like we have much choice anyway, with the short time we have left."

Becky nodded. "Yep, that's all we can do. See if James needs any help, but make sure you get some sleep tonight, OK? We need you awake tomorrow night at the dance."

The Valentine's Day Project *Disaster*

18.Love Me...Not

Amanda and Becky were busy chatting as they walked into math class on V-day - February 14. They were so absorbed in their conversation that Susan had to poke Amanda three times to get her attention.

"Oww!" What was *that* for?" demanded Amanda, rubbing her shoulder.

Love Me...Not

Susan didn't say anything; she just pointed towards Amanda's desk. Amanda turned and followed Susan's finger. There was a box of chocolates tied up with a big bow, sitting on top of an envelope in the center of her desk.

"I wonder who that's from?" asked Becky.

"I don't know, and *I don't care*," said Amanda, stomping over to the desk and picking up the box and the envelope. She walked straight over to the teacher's desk and dropped them into the rubbish bin. "They're probably from *him*."

Susan shrugged and walked over to the bin. She fished out the box. "You sure you don't want these? It looks like they might be nice..."

Amanda shook her head firmly. "You can have them, I don't care. I don't want anything from Oliver. I *hate him!*"

"A *little drastic*, maybe," said Becky, helping Susan untie the bow. "Besides, you only know what you saw; maybe you got it all wrong."

Amanda shook her head again. "I know what I saw."

"What are you going to do if someone finds the card and opens it?" asked Susan as she lifted the lid off the box of chocolates. "Oooooh, these look *expensive*. They're all fancy chocolates with caramels and fillings and stuff."

160

The Valentine's Day Project *Disaster*

Panic swept across Amanda's face as she ran to the bin and grabbed the envelope. "You're right, *nobody* can find this. I'll have to get rid of it later." She stuffed the envelope into her backpack and zipped it shut.

"You sure you don't want some?" Becky asked through chocolate-covered lips. "They're really good."

Amanda shook her head again. "Nope, for all I know he *poisoned* them or something."

Susan choked and spat out a half-chewed caramel into her hand. "What, no, really, people don't *do* that, do they? Like, this is just middle school."

Becky kept chewing and licked her lips. "Nothing wrong with these chocolates. Mmmm-mmm, delicious!"

"Who they *came from* is what's wrong," muttered Amanda.

"Seems to me if he didn't like you, he wouldn't be buying you fancy chocolates like this," said Becky. "Besides, are you sure they're from him?"

"I..." began Amanda, "...I...who else would they be from?"

"I dunno, the whole school knows you by now," said Susan, picking out a mint chocolate. "Becky was getting invites even after she'd asked Chip, maybe you have a secret admirer or something? Weirder stuff can happen at Valentine's."

"Really? You think so?" Amanda brightened, fumbling with the zip on her bag. She pulled out the envelope and examined the writing. She sighed, and then dropped the card back into her bag. "Nah, looks like Olly's writing."

"Too bad," said Susan, stuffing the last chocolate into her mouth. "The chocolates were really good."

"Speaking of chocolate," said Amanda, "what did you get, Becky?"

"Ah, I haven't seen Chip yet today. But I got him a card and two rolls of candy hearts," Becky shrugged, looking into Amanda's open backpack. "Not nearly as big as that card though. Man, Oliver must really like you. Maybe you should talk to him."

Amanda sighed. "I don't know what to do. Maybe you're right." She pulled the empty box towards her and picked out a couple of crumbs of chocolate.

"You're right, that was nice chocolate. Did you two *have* to eat them so fast?" groaned Amanda, glancing at Susan and Becky. "That was like watching a vacuum cleaner."

Becky licked her fingers. "Couldn't pass up the opportunity. Besides, who knows how quickly you might come back to your senses?"

Amanda sighed. "Oh well, too late now. Maybe you can share one of yours when you get some from Chip."

Becky raised an eyebrow then shrugged. "Yeah, sure. Or whatever he gives me."

The morning went by quickly, with lots of cards and candies being exchanged in classrooms and hallways. As soon as the lunch bell rang, the three girls headed straight to the gym. Alice and the boys were already waiting by the gym door, as their bell had rung a few minutes earlier. The eight children worked quickly, setting up the tables & chairs and hanging streamers while James tested the sound system.

"They cancelled all of the gym classes this afternoon, so we can leave everything setup. The custodian will be hanging the mirror ball and black lights right after lunch, and he will set up some colored spotlights around the gym walls. We'll put out the food right after school, and then the teachers will do the judging of the decorations and the baking right after that," said Amanda.

"Will the decorations and baking be *safe?*" asked Tim, a frown creasing his forehead.

Susan nodded. "Yup, the principal said they'll lock up the gym right after the judging. We can go home right after we put out the food and stuff, so we can get ready. Everything will be perfectly safe."

Alice smiled. "That's good to hear. We don't need any more problems."

"Speaking of trouble, has anyone seen Pete lately?" asked James.

"Someone said he might be sick today," said Susan.

"I hope he gets better soon," said Becky.

Amanda frowned. "Really? After all he's done?"

Becky sighed. "Sorry, automatic reaction. But still, I hope he's not *too* sick."

"Well, that's good news for us if he is," said Susan as the bell began to ring. "Less of a chance for him to cause us any more trouble."

"Well, time to get back to class, we'll see you tonight!" waved Ben.

The afternoon classes flashed by in a blur. Math, social studies, English - and then the final bell rang. It had barely finished ringing when the students flowed out into the hallways, lingering only long enough to empty their lockers on the way out the door. It seemed that almost everyone was going to the dance - and those that hadn't bought tickets were having second thoughts.

The Valentine's Day Project *Disaster*

Amanda met Becky and Susan just outside the locked closet that held most of the food. Amanda glanced around the hallway as the last few students trickled out of the front doors.

"Umm... how are we going to get all of the food into the gym? There are a lot of containers to carry," said Amanda.

"All sorted!" called out Chip as he came around the corner, steering two kitchen trolleys in front of him, one with each hand. "These will let us get the food moved and setup in no time."

"Good choice, Becky," said Susan, nudging her arm. "Cute, and a thinker too!"

Becky stuck out her tongue at Susan, then walked over to help Chip with the carts. One had a wobbly wheel and kept pulling to the left.

"Thanks, Becky," grinned Chip.

Amanda grunted and unlocked the closet door. Within moments, they started loading up the first trolley.

When it was close to full, Becky volunteered to take the first cart to the gym with Chip. "It should work faster if we have someone there unloading and someone running back and forth with the carts."

Amanda nodded, and handed Susan two plastic containers of cookies. Susan stacked the containers on the bottom shelf of the second cart, three containers high.

Two minutes later, Chip came zooming around the corner with an empty cart. "Ready for the next one!"

Susan placed the final container on the top and nodded to Chip. "Drive slower than you came here, we can't afford to have any broken baking," she warned.

After several more trips they moved on to the next closet and loaded up the soft drinks. When the last cart was loaded, they all went into the gym to help Becky finish setting up the tables.

"Almost four o'clock," said Amanda, putting the last soft drink bottle under a table. "I'll go tell the principal they can start the judging. You three can head on home and start getting ready. We've only got an hour and a half until the dance starts!"

"*Nothing* can go wrong now," commented Amanda as she closed the front door of her house. She took her shoes off and walked up the stairs and into the kitchen. Ben was setting the table for an early dinner. He was already dressed for the dance, his hair still wet from being washed and freshly brushed.

"You look different," said Amanda.

Ben froze. He pointed the fork in his right hand like a weapon. "What do you mean by that?"

"What? Oh, nothing. I mean, you look good. Not like…normal," said Amanda, taking a step back.

Ben scowled.

"You know, all tidy and ready for the dance, that's all I mean," sighed Amanda.

Ben grunted, then placed the fork on the table. "You'd better hurry up, dinner's in fifteen minutes."

"I'm having a quick shower first. Rushing to do all that setup made us sweaty," said Amanda as she walked out of the kitchen.

"Good thing too, 'cos you *stink!*" called out Ben as he started filling glasses with water.

"Have fun at the dance, you two," said Mrs. Jones as Amanda walked down the front step. Ben was already standing by the curb, motioning for Amanda to hurry up.

"We will, thanks Mom!" said Amanda as she hurried to catch up with her brother, who had already crossed the street into the park. "Hey, wait for me!"

Ben slowed but didn't stop. Amanda caught up with him and poked him in the arm. "Hey, we're not supposed to get sweaty *before* the dance!"

Love Me...Not

Ben grunted and resumed walking at his normal pace. "So, everything ready to go?" he asked.

"Yup, decorations, food, drinks are all good, and the principal said she would lock everything up after the judging so there should be no problems," said Amanda, ticking off the fingers on her left hand. "And apparently Pete is sick or something, so now all we have to do is enjoy the dance!"

They walked the rest of the way in silence. The rounded gravel crunched loudly as they walked across the school yard to the main building entrance. They went inside to find the place packed with dressed-up kids chatting in small groups. Amanda and Ben worked their way through the crowded hallway until they came to the gym doors.

"Just in time," commented Tim. "We were worried you were going to be late. You're the last ones to get here."

"Somebody had to have a shower 'cos she stunk," said Ben, earning him another poke in the arm.

"Now all we're waiting for is the principal to unlock the door," said Tim.

"It had better be soon," remarked Susan. The buzz of conversation was getting louder, and the restless students were beginning to move closer to the gym doors. A row of teachers standing along the side kept them from pushing in too close.

"Excuse me please, *excuse me!*" called out a familiar voice. A few moments later, they could see

The Valentine's Day Project *Disaster*

Ms. Moldiva working her way through the crowd of children. As she came closer, the crowd melted away in front of her, leaving an empty space in front of the doors.

"A very good evening, yes?" smiled Ms. Moldiva as she reached into her pocket for a set of keys. "I am very pleased with vot you children have done. A very good project, yes - a very good project."

Becky grinned, and nodded at Chip.

Ms. Moldiva fumbled with the keys for a few moments until she found the correct one. She raised her hand in the air, waiting for silence as conversations slowly stopped.

"I am very pleased with all of you children, for supporting our school and zee organizers of zee dance," called out Ms. Moldiva. "Now, I hope you all have a vonderful evening."

With that, she motioned Amanda forward. She handed Amanda the keys, and smiled. "I think you should be doing zee honors, yes? You children have vorked very hard."

Amanda accepted the keys, and slowly slid the key into the lock. She turned the key until heard the deadbolt slide clear of the door. She slowly withdrew the key from the lock, and handed the keys back to Ms. Moldiva.

Amanda glanced over her shoulder at Susan. "Here goes nothing!" she whispered as she swung the doors open.

Love Me...Not

The gym lights were off. Darkness filled the room, with only a thin shaft of light reaching into the room from the doorway. Amanda walked into the darkness, a few steps to the left. She fumbled around briefly, feeling for the light switch panel. She flipped the top three switches.

The lights over the stage flickered and began to glow softly as they warmed up. Several colored spotlights began reflecting off of the slowly rotating mirror ball.

However, it was the single spotlight shining down onto the center of the floor that caught everyone's attention.

Decorations lay scattered around the room.

And in the center of it all, the light casting a long shadow behind him, stood Pimple Pete.

19.Sweet Revenge

"Hah!" yelled Pete. He had his hands on his hips, feet spread wide and his jaw stuck out defiantly. "Let's see if you can have your stupid dance now, with no decorations!"

Amanda began to see red. "**How? Who? How could you!** Where did you come from? You're supposed to be *sick!*"

"He's *sick* all right," said Chip, taking a step toward Pete, smacking his left hand with his right fist. "But not as sick as he's gonna be."

A cold, thin hand gripped his shoulder, holding him back. "Just vait, young man," said Ms. Moldiva, shaking her head. She turned to face the crowd of children in the hallway who were craning to see what was going on. Several girls gasped and covered their mouths, while a number of the boys began forming fists.

171

Sweet Revenge

The principal's voice rang out. "I am very sorry, it would appear zat someone has ruined all of your decorations." She glared at the lone figure in the middle of the room. "I will be dealing vith *him* later."

"But what do we do *now?*" wailed Amanda, fighting back tears.

"I'll show you what we'll do," growled Chip, as he pulled free from Ms. Moldiva's grip.

The hand that grabbed his arm next was small and warm. Chip turned in surprise to see Becky holding him back. "Not that way," she shook her head. She let go of his arm and took his hand. "Follow me."

Chip let Becky lead him into the gym. She made her way slowly around the room until she bent over and picked up a decoration with her free hand. "Ours."

She led Chip over to a nearby wall and stuck the decoration to the wall with a bit of torn tape. She made a point of ignoring Pete as she led Chip around the room, looking for the next decoration.

Becky glanced towards the doorway as she fastened the second decoration to a pillar. A few other children entered the gym, walking slowly around the room, eyes searching. Every one of them avoided looking at Pete.

As the third child picked up a decoration, the smirk on Pete's face began to disappear. He looked around the room as a growing number of children entered the gym, searching the floor. "Mine", "Ours", "Mine" echoed out throughout the gym as decorations were picked up and fastened to the walls and pillars. Every single person ignored Pete - it was like he didn't even exist.

Sweet Revenge

The smirk now completely absent, Pete began waving his hands. "Hey! Over here! Aren't you going to yell or anything?"

Children continued to ignore Pete as they worked their way around the room. Becky and Chip walked up onto the stage, their final decoration found and repaired. James was already there, plugging in his MP3 player into the sound system. Moments later, fast-paced music began to play through the speakers, drowning out Pete's voice.

Large open spaces appeared on the floor as the decorations were picked up. Slowly at first, children began dancing in twos and threes until fifty, then a hundred children were dancing throughout the gym.

All except for the middle of the room, where Pete stood all alone, in a large empty circle. Everyone continued to ignore him.

Everyone, that is - except for a tall woman with bony fingers, beckoning for him to leave the gym.

Amanda was selling cookies at the bake sale table when someone tapped her on the shoulder. She turned, surprised to see Oliver standing behind her.

The Valentine's Day Project *Disaster*

"What do *you* want?" she demanded, yelling over the loud music.

"You didn't wait!" he yelled back, cupping his hand around his mouth.

"What?" yelled Amanda, as the song boomed louder.

"Can we talk?" yelled Oliver, motioning toward the gym door.

Amanda shrugged, tapped Susan on the shoulder, and then stood up. Oliver waited for her to clear the table, then they walked slowly together towards the gym door.

Once out in the hallway, the sounds of the loud music faded as the door swung shut. Amanda turned to face Oliver, hands on her hips. "So what do you want?"

Oliver looked hurt. "You didn't wait."

"What do you mean, I didn't wait? What for?" demanded Amanda.

"Didn't you get my card?" asked Oliver slowly. "If someone else took it, I'll find out who it was..."

Amanda waved her hand. "Yeah, I got it. So?"

Oliver looked briefly confused, then annoyed. "I came to your house, but you had already left. I told you I was going to meet you, I wrote it in the card."

"Why would you do that?" asked Amanda.

175

Sweet Revenge

"Why - because we were going to the dance together!" stammered Oliver. "Did you get the chocolates? Did you like them?"

Amanda grunted. "Yeah, I got 'em. Becky and Susan ate them."

Oliver frowned. "They weren't for them, they were for *you!*"

Amanda stared at the ground, gritting her teeth. "I didn't want them. I was mad."

"Why?"

"*You know why,*" growled Amanda.

"No, I don't," said Oliver, his frown deepening.

"Ugh. Boys are so *stupid*," Amanda took a deep breath. "I-am-mad-at-you-because-you-gave-my-ticket-to-that-little-blonde-girl!"

"**Oh!**" Oliver took a step back. "Oh! Well, that was…that was nothing."

"***Nothing?!***" hissed Amanda. "I saw you give her ***my*** ticket, and then ***she kissed you!***"

"What? No way, I mean, yes she kissed me on the cheek, but I didn't *ask* for it, and…well, it wasn't *your* ticket anyway. It was *hers.*"

Amanda took a deep breath, her face reddening.

Before she could explode, Oliver quickly added "I didn't need to buy you a ticket, the organizers go

176

for free. You didn't need a ticket! Didn't the principal tell you?"

Amanda paused, looked him in the eye, and said "Well, that may be so, but why did you buy *her* a ticket anyway? I mean, she kissed you and *everything!*"

Oliver took a deep, slow breath. "Jessica really wanted to go to the dance, right? But her grandmother just died, and her family was heading out of town to the funeral *that afternoon*, and they weren't going to be back until today. She didn't want to miss out on the dance, so she gave me some money so I could get her ticket before she left for the funeral."

Amanda blinked twice. "**Oh**."

Oliver shuffled his feet. "Yeah."

"So she kissed you because…" began Amanda.

"Heck if I know, she was pretty emotional about her Grandma dying, I think she was just happy someone would do her a favor at the time, you know?"

"So…you don't *like* her then?" said Amanda slowly.

"Well, yeah, sure, I guess I like her, she's a friend of the family, but more like a sister really," said Oliver. "We almost grew up together, you know, since we were little."

177

Sweet Revenge

"Ohhhhh," said Amanda, visibly deflating. She covered her face with her hands and started to cry. "I'm such a *mean, horrible* person!"

"What? No, it was just a misunderstanding, really, *anybody* could have made that mistake," said Oliver, awkwardly patting her on the shoulder.

Amanda shook her head. "No, it's *all my fault*, I pushed you away, I was so *mad*...I haven't even opened your card yet. I threw it out, but then I thought someone might open it, which would be *worse*, so I stuffed it in my bag..."

Oliver stuck out his bottom lip. "Threw it out, huh? Well, I guess you thought...well, it doesn't matter now."

"I'm so sorry, Olly," said Amanda, hugging him hard. "Can you forgive me?"

Oliver cautiously hugged her back. "Um, sure. Let's go get a cookie and then dance or something."

Amanda released Oliver and wiped her face with the side of her hand. She gave him a shy smile, and shook her head.

Oliver frowned. "What? After all that, you don't want to dance or anything?"

Amanda shook her head again. "*Yes* to the cookie and *yes* to the dance. But first, *we* need to do something else." She took his hand and began to lead him down the hallway towards the school office.

"Um, where are we going?" asked Oliver.

"We need to ask Ms. Moldiva to open up the craft room. We never made a decoration together."

"**Oh!**" said Oliver.

Sweet Revenge

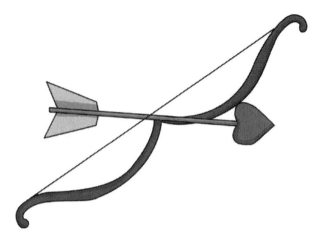

20. Just Desserts

"That was an awesome dance," said Susan the next day after school, where they had all gathered at Tim and Tom's house for the lessons-learned session. "Adam was actually a pretty good dancer."

"Well, apparently you were too, because I saw you dance with him *four* times," smiled Becky.

181

Just Desserts

"Yeah, and didn't he buy you some cake and a soft drink, too?" said Amanda, with a sly grin.

Susan blushed. "Yes, well, but I bought him a muffin, so it was even."

"Uh-huh," nodded Becky and Amanda together. "So you *like* him, huh?"

Susan tried to suppress a smile. "Yeah, well, he's OK, I guess. At least at dancing."

Ben and Tom pretended to throw up.

"Speaking of *dancing*," interrupted Becky, "Didn't I see you dancing with *Tim*, Alice?"

Alice blushed. "Yeah, well, it just seemed the right thing to do, you know? Setting a good example, getting people out onto the dance floor, that kind of thing."

"Uh-huh," said Becky. "It looked like the floor was pretty full already. So - was he any good?"

"He did alright, considering he said he didn't know how to dance," said Alice, glancing shyly at Tim.

"Some robot-man," said Susan. "I saw him smiling and laughing. And I even saw him *hold your hand!*"

Tim coughed. "Excuse me, *robot boy* right here. That was just for the *pirouette*, you know, spinning? I had to hold her hand to spin Alice around. It was just part of the dance, OK?"

"Yeah, sure Mr. Spock - or should I say *Valentino*?" Amanda winked. "Looks like you actually studied up for that dance."

"Um, well, I practiced with my Mom a little bit, but it was easier with Alice because she's the right size for me, you know - the perfect fit - I mean..." stammered Tim, freckles disappearing into his reddening cheeks.

"It was just a dance, that's all, we're just *friends*," said Alice firmly.

"That's right," said Tim, nodding as he broke a cookie in two and offered half to Alice. "Just friends."

Alice nodded, accepting the half-cookie. "*Only* friends."

"Oh man," groaned Ben.

"Well...anyway..." said Becky, shaking her head, "I think James actually did a pretty good job with the music."

James grinned.

"Hey! *I* was *accountable* for the music," protested Susan. "It was my job, don't I get some thanks too?"

Amanda shook her head. "Give credit where credit is due. You did a good job on the quality checking, but James did a great job putting it all together. Especially on the 'slow' dances. It was brilliant!"

Just Desserts

Susan glanced at James. "Well, I have to admit he had me worried with all of that 'trust me' stuff, but James really pulled it off. I mean, who would have thought you could take a song, and slow it down *four* times - and then mash it up with a normal speed song and make it work?" she shook her head.

"You were brilliant at that part," Alice nodded at James.

Becky nodded. "Yep, it was cool. And I'm glad to see that you and Oliver sorted things out - I mean, **ouch** - *you* got sorted out," said Becky, as Amanda elbowed her in the arm.

"Well, let's get started on writing down the lessons we learned, so we can try and get finished before the pizza arrives," said Tim.

"Right!" said Alice, paper and pen ready. "So what did we learn?"

"Lots of stuff, really," said James. "Organizing a dance is really hard, but the hardest part is the people."

"Right, that stuff Amanda's dad said about *advocates* and learning how to *influence* people was really important," said Susan.

"As long as you do it the right way and are *honest* about it - those *rumors* nearly wrecked everything," muttered Becky.

The Valentine's Day Project *Disaster*

"The contest for the baking and decorations worked really well," said Amanda, nodding at Tim. "But it only really started to work once we got some *advocates* to help us."

"It was nice of that dentist to give out more passes to Mega Play World for the prizes," sighed Ben. "I wish I could have won them."

"We weren't allowed to win anything anyway, 'cos we organized the dance," said Alice. "It would look like we cheated."

"Which leads up to...people will usually help when you are *honest*, and they understand and agree with what you are trying to do," said Tom.

Amanda nodded. "Yeah, the planning and scheduling stuff seemed simple compared to the rest of it. If we hadn't had the help of the advocates, the plan wouldn't have mattered - sure the dance may have happened, but maybe with only a few people there. It would have been a real disaster for sure."

"Don't forget, we still needed to break things down into small pieces," said Tim. "So we could manage it all without going crazy. You always have to do that."

Ben grinned. "We had a lot of crazy people on this project - crazy with looove...**ow!**"

Amanda and Becky slowly put their hands back on the table.

Just Desserts

"But it's really important that you have the right message, and you approach people the right way," sighed Susan. "No yelling at people - ever, 'cos you never know when you may need their help."

"And you have to be prepared to take some risks," said Becky. "I wasn't sure if Chip was going to say yes. That was a little scary."

"I'm glad I did," said Chip, smiling at Becky. "This dance was a lot more fun than last year."

"And...you have to try and not *jump to conclusions*, right, Amanda?" asked Oliver, a serious expression on his face.

Amanda flushed red. "Yeah, I'm really sorry about that, Olly."

Oliver smiled. "Me too. Maybe on the next project we can all work together?"

Amanda looked around the table at her friends.

"As long as it's not another *dance*, fine with me," said Susan.

Tim and Tom shrugged. Ben nodded. James gave Oliver a thumbs up.

Alice nodded. "Oliver, you're OK. I'd be happy to work with you next time."

"What about Chip?" asked Becky. "He worked hard on this project. He should be allowed to help next time too. If he *wants* to, that is."

Chip nodded. "We'll see what kind of project it is, first."

"Couldn't have done this one without you," grinned Amanda. "*Advocate number one!* We owe a lot to you for helping make this dance a success."

"I'd settle for the first slice of pepperoni," said Chip, as Tim and Tom's father placed a stack of steaming hot pizza boxes on the kitchen table. "Let's eat!"

"Too bad about Pete," said Becky as she bit into her fourth slice of pizza.

"Yeah, well, litter pickup for the rest of the year seems to be a pretty small punishment," sniffed Alice. "What he did was *really, really* mean."

"Yeah, maybe, but that's not his *only* punishment," said Chip.

"Why, what else did the principal give him? *Detention?*" scoffed Susan. "That's fine if she did that too."

Chip shook his head. "No, I mean *the punishment from the rest of the school. Nobody* is talking to him at all now - except the teachers, but I guess they kind of have to. It's really pretty horrible, when you think about it."

"Yeah, so?" shrugged Amanda. "He deserves it."

Just Desserts

Becky shook her head. "Sure, he's a bully, and he did some mean things. But it doesn't mean he's actually *evil*."

Susan shook her head. "He seems pretty bad to me."

"There are lots of reasons someone can act like a bully, maybe they are pushed around at home, or by other kids. Sometimes they just want attention," said Becky.

"Well, he won't be getting any of that for a while, so he had better get used to it," said Amanda.

"Sometimes being yelled at is better than not being yelled at. In this case, everyone is ignoring him, it's like he *doesn't even exist*. How would you like it if everyone around you didn't pay any attention to you, at all - for weeks and weeks?" asked Becky.

Susan shifted uncomfortably in her seat. "Um…I wouldn't like it so much, I guess. It would get pretty hard after a while."

Chip nodded. "I agree that Pete needs punishment, and some time to think hard about what he's done and how it hurt lots of people."

Becky took a deep breath. "*I* think…after a couple of weeks, it will have been enough time. Not the litter pickup, I mean the *people ignoring* him part. That will have to stop, or he may actually turn evil."

Susan raised an eyebrow. "So how do you propose to get people to *not* ignore him? They're pretty mad right now."

Becky frowned. "I'm not sure what we can do about other people, I mean just *us*. *We* are going to have to talk to him. Figure out why he's been acting like a jerk. And maybe…"

"Maybe what?" asked Amanda.

"…Maybe, just maybe, we might end up making a new friend," said Becky.

"As if *we* could ever be friends with *him!*" said Amanda.

"You never know," said Alice, "stranger things have happened. Just look at you and Oliver - you used to hate him!"

Oliver raised an eyebrow.

"But that's *different!*" protested Amanda. "He was just trying to get my attention!"

"And how is Pete so different?" asked Becky. "We don't know why he behaved like a jerk; it could be the same kind of thing."

"I don't know…" began Amanda.

"I think we need to find out," said Tim, looking at Chip. "He's not *always* a jerk; I mean you were his friend, right?"

Just Desserts

Chip nodded. "Yeah, we were friends - are friends still, I guess. He's not really so bad most of the time."

"So there is some hope then," said Becky.

Chip shrugged. "I guess there's always hope."

Tim nodded. "Right then, mark the calendar for two weeks."

Susan frowned. "Mark it for what?"

"The start of our *next* project," declared Tim.

Amanda raised an eyebrow. "And that is what, exactly?"

"To see if we can un-bully a bully," said Tim. "I think it's worth a try."

"Me too," said Becky.

Chip nodded. "I'm in."

"I think we learned a lot about working with people this time. We might need some more help, but I think we can do it," said Alice.

Amanda threw up her hands. "I give up! I don't think it'll ever work!"

"Well, maybe not, but you know what they say," said Becky.

"What's that?" frowned Amanda.

"Keep your friends close," said Becky, "but keep your enemies closer."

Did you like this book? Please leave a comment or review.

Check out the website for fun activities and projects!

www.projectkidsadventures.com

Just Desserts

Project Kids Adventures

The Easter Bully Transformation Project

The Project Kids really have their work cut out for themselves this time. After Peter Johansen nearly destroyed the Valentine's Dance, you might expect the Project Kids to be glad to see the last of 'Pimple Pete'. So why are they reaching out to him - and what do they hope to achieve?

As one small idea takes on a life of its own and one of their own is struck down in their prime, they find themselves struggling to answer one simple question: Can they actually *un-bully* a bully? ...And should they even *try?*

The answer lies in an unexpected place...and not even the Easter Bunny can help them.

Coming Soon

Parent/Teacher Note:

The next book in the Project Kids Adventures series sees the kids tackling several interrelated projects at once.

While carefully investigating the reasons behind Pimple Pete's bullying behavior, they find themselves engaged in a cause that extends well beyond the school and their community.

The Project Kids Team

James Cartwright

Age: 11

Height: 57 inches (145cm)

Eyes: Brown

Hair: Dark Blonde

Likes: Comic books, Computer games, Building stuff, Campfires, Becky

Dislikes: New shoes, Spiders, Going to dances alone, Vampires

Skills: Running, Climbing, Swimming, Music

More info: www.projectkidsadventures.com/James

The Project Kids Team

Ben Jones

Age: 11

Height: 59 inches (150cm)

Eyes: Brown

Hair: Dark Brown

Likes: Being in charge, Chocolate

Dislikes: Big sisters, Bullies

Skills: Building stuff, Driving remote control robots

More info: www.projectkidsadventures.com/Ben

Tim O'Reilly

Age: 11

Height: 56 inches (142cm)

Eyes: Green

Hair: Red (Curly)

Likes: Drawing, Planning

Dislikes: Bullies, Not having a plan

Skills: Working together, Planning, Lateral thinker

More info:

www.projeckidsadventures.com/Tim

Tom O'Reilly

Age: 11

Height: 56 inches (142cm)

Eyes: Green

Hair: Red (Curly)

Likes: Computer games, Camping

Dislikes: Splinters, People who argue

Skills: Building stuff, Teamwork

More info:

www.projectkidsadventures.com/Tom

Amanda Jones

Age: 12

Height: 60 inches (152 cm)

Eyes: Green

Hair: Dark Brown

Likes: Teamwork, Oliver, Girl Guides

Dislikes: Bossy people, Bullies

Skills: Planning, Setting goals, Leadership, Nice writing

More info:

www.projectkidsadventures.com/Amanda

The Project Kids Team

Susan Cartwright

Age: 12

Height: 59 inches (149 cm)

Eyes: Blue

Hair: Blonde

Likes: Nature, hiking

Dislikes: Little brothers, Stubborn boys

Skills: Planning, Communicating

More info: www.projectkidsadventures.com/Susan

Becky Petrov

Age: 12

Height: 58 inches (147cm)

Eyes: Brown

Hair: Brown

Likes: James, Chip, Chocolate

Dislikes: People arguing

Skills: Speaking to crowds, Peacemaker

More info: www.projectkidsadventures.com/Becky

Alice Wong

Age: 11

Height: 56 inches (142cm)

Eyes: Brown

Hair: Black

Likes: Cooperating with others, Drawing, Playing with her friends

Dislikes: Messes, Cupid

Skills: Drawing and sketching, Organizing things

More info: www.projectkidsadventures.com/Alice

Other Kids

Charles (Chip) Cooper

Age: 13

Height: 63 inches (160 cm)

Eyes: Blue

Hair: Blonde

Likes: Helping others, Becky, Soccer

Dislikes: Being bossed around

Oliver Winston

Age: 12

Height: 60 inches (152 cm)

Eyes: Blue

Hair: Blonde

Likes: Mice, Amanda, Computers

Dislikes: People jumping to conclusions

Peter Johansen

Age: 13

Height: 65 inches (165 cm)

Eyes: Brown

Hair: Brown

Likes: Running things, Getting his own way

Dislikes: Stubborn people, Little kids

Todd Morgan

Age: 13

Height: 63 inches (160 cm)

Eyes: Brown

Hair: Brown

Likes: Video games, Hanging out with friends

Dislikes: Bossy girls, Yelling

The Project Kids Team

Glossary

ACCOUNTABILITY – The person who is *accountable* for a task has to make sure that it gets done right. Susan was accountable to Tim to deliver the music. However, Susan *delegated* the job of selecting the dance music to James, so James was *responsible* for selecting the music. However, Susan had to do *quality control* on the music to make sure it was a good selection.

Note: If you are assigned a task to work on, you are both *responsible* to do the task, and *accountable* for the results (i.e. doing a good job). You can *delegate responsibility* (i.e. assign the task to someone else, like a boss does), but you cannot *delegate accountability*.

ADVOCATE – An *advocate* (sometimes called a Champion) believes in what you are trying to do, and actively seeks to help you and your cause.

Glossary

A successful advocate usually has *influence* with a group or groups of people, and can help you communicate a message to a wider audience, particularly when there may be initial resistance to your message. The *advocate* might be considered an expert in something, is usually a great communicator and may also be fun to hang around with.

The advocate uses their *network* of people to help communicate the message to lots of people, and get them engaged. Having *advocates* is a very important thing when you are trying to get people to change (i.e. *Change Management*) - in this case, change the minds of the other children to come to the dance, create decorations and bring food.

The opposite of an *advocate* is an *antagonist*.

ANTAGONIST – While an *advocate* is actively helping to promote something, an *antagonist* will be trying to stop it, prevent it from happening, or make things difficult for the people who are working on the project. Pimple Pete was clearly an antagonist in this story, and was trying to interfere with the dance and try to stop it from happening - unless *he* was allowed to run it.

BUDGET – The budget is what you plan to spend on your project. There may also be some *income* to consider, but mostly the budget is for planning what you need to spend money on to have a successful project. For the dance, the project kids had a lot of ideas for what they needed to buy to run the dance, but the money they wanted to spend was more than they were being allowed to spend by the principal. That is why they had to *prioritize* the list of things they wanted to buy - so the important stuff would be bought first, and so on through the list, until they ran out of money.

CHANGE MANAGEMENT – Convincing people to try new things, do things differently or simply change their minds about something takes a lot of effort. People don't usually like change, but it is a part of everyday life. *Change Management* is a very important part of any project that involves people. In the Valentine's Dance project, the kids begin to learn some aspects of change management as they work with *stakeholders* (all of the kids at the school) to try and convince them to attend the dance, create decorations and bring in baking.

CLOSEOUT Phase (Finish Up) – This is the end of the project, where we make sure that everything we wanted to do for the project is complete.

CONCURRENT Tasks – Tasks that need to happen at the same time.

CONTROL Phase (Lead, Check & Correct) – This is checking that we are still working to the plan, and making corrections if we start to wander off or get distracted by other things. It also includes working with people to make sure they have what they need to get their tasks done, and that people are getting along. The Project Manager spends a fair bit of time doing this.

Glossary

CRITICAL PATH – This is the longest path in your sequence diagram, when you add up the *estimated durations* of each task.

CROWDSOURCING – Getting help from many people in small ways, to help you accomplish something big. It could be fundraising, or getting baking and decorations done for a dance. Crowdsourcing often involves a small token of appreciation being given to the giver (like a Hershey's Kiss), and sometimes there are larger gift draws or prizes.

DELEGATION – This involves getting other people to help you get things done. On most projects, you can't do it all yourself, so you need to assign (*delegate*) parts of the work to other people. Effective delegating is a good leadership skill, but you also need to make sure things get done properly, so delegate tasks to people you think will do a good job on that particular task. For example, most of the drawing on the projects was *delegated* to Alice, because she was good at it.

(Also see ***accountability*** and ***responsibility***)

DELIVERABLE – This is something you are trying to achieve or build with your project - a completed piece of work. This may be small or big, but it is something you can see and measure. When you finish with a key **task**, the result will often be a deliverable. Examples of deliverables are: music, decorations, food, drinks, tickets, flyers, etc.

DEPENDENCY – When one activity (or task) cannot start until another one is finished, there is a dependency on the first task. In the diagram (A->B), B cannot start before A finished because B is dependent on A.

DURATION – This is how long a task takes to complete. If it has not started yet or is not finished, it is an *estimated duration*. If the task is finished, you know the *actual duration* - how long it really took to finish it.

ESTIMATED DURATION – How long you think it will take to finish something.

EXECUTION Phase (Do) – This is when the "real" work of the project begins, and most of the building/doing activity happens.

EXPENSE – Money you spend. The dance needed some money to be spent on decorations, and food and drinks that would be sold at the dance.

EXTRINISIC (EXTERNAL) MOTIVATION – This comes from **external** factors that may *motivate* you to behave in a particular way. External factors often include rewards, such as the promise of food, money, free time, special activities etc. External factors are visible to other people. External motivation factors can also be related to punishment - such as doing something to *avoid* getting into trouble. (i.e. "do this, or else I will tell on you!")

Glossary

External motivation factors often produce temporary results, and the person may go back to doing things their own way once they receive the 'reward'. *(See chapter 11 for a detailed discussion on motivation).*

GANTT CHART - A way of showing the project plan with Tasks, Schedule, Resources and Dependencies on the page all at once. This is one of the most popular and useful ways of showing project activities displayed against time.

INCOME – Money you earn. The money COMEs IN to you. The school earned money from the ticket sales (before the dance) and the sales of food and drink (during the dance).

INFLUENCE – Influence is the ability to have an effect on other people, which may affect their behavior, how they think, and what they do. Quite often children (and some adults) will copy the behaviors and actions of influential role models, such as parents, rock stars, etc.

Note: There are positive and negative types of influence; *negative* would be to try and convince someone to do something bad or unhealthy (like stealing or smoking), while positive influences are generally good, teaching you to help other people, be honest, exercise regularly, etc.

INITIATION Phase (Idea/Think) – In the Initiation phase of the project, we have an idea about what we want to accomplish – what we want to do. ("Let's build a tree house!")

INTRINSIC (INTERNAL) MOTIVATION – This comes from **internal** factors that may *motivate* you to behave in a particular way. The internal factors are not visible to other people, but usually have you feeling good (a sense of satisfaction, or 'warm fuzzies') when you accomplish a goal or do a good job at something.

Intrinsic motivation is far more powerful and long-lasting than external motivation factors. *(See chapter 11 for a detailed discussion on motivation)*.

LESSONS LEARNED SESSION – At the end of the project (and in the middle of long projects), the team meets to talk about what parts went well, which did not go so well and discuss ideas on how they might do things better next time.

MOTIVATION – The reason or reasons for acting in a particular way or doing certain things. The project kids had to figure out how to *motivate* the other kids in the school to *want* to go to the dance.

PLANNING Phase (Plan) – During the planning phase of the project, we figure out what needs to be done - in detail - and decide how we are going to do it. ("What do we need for the dance, and how will we do it?")

PROJECT – A project is a temporary activity with a defined goal, a beginning and an end.

PROJECT MANAGEMENT – Project Management is the application of knowledge, skills, tools and techniques to project activities to meet the project requirements.

PROJECT SPONSOR – This person is the one who wants the project to happen, and has given approval for the project to proceed. The sponsor usually sets out guidelines for the project, which may include the *Budget*, *Scope* and other factors. The project sponsor is a key decision-maker on your project. In the case of the Valentine's Dance, this is the first project that the Project Kids have done for someone else, and the ultimate decisions were made by Ms. Moldiva (who could help with the project, what the budget was, where it would be held, increasing the budget for the shopping list when ticket sales were doing very well).

QUALITY CONTROL – This is an important part of every project, and helps to make sure that what you are delivering or building is done right, and is safe, etc. On the Tree House project, the parents did quality control checks during the safety inspection, and the kids checked each level to make sure it was safe before starting on the next level up. On the Valentine's Dance project, Susan had to do quality control checking on the music selection.

REQUIREMENTS – What do we want to have as the results of our project? Some of the requirements for the science fair were provided by the teacher.

RESPONSIBILITY – Whoever is assigned a task is *responsible* for their part of the work. This may be a part of the project that they do on their own, or they may be doing it as part of a team. James was *responsible* for selecting the music, because Susan had *delegated* the task to him and he accepted it. However, the task was originally assigned to Susan by Tim, so she was *accountable* for making sure the music was delivered.

Note: If you are assigned a task to work on, you are both *responsible* to do the task, and *accountable* for the results (i.e. doing a good job). You can *delegate responsibility* (i.e assign the task to someone else, like a boss does) but you cannot *delegate accountability*.

RESOURCES – Materials, tools, people or money needed to complete the project. The Project Kids team has eight people, they used wood for the maze, they used tools to measure time, they had the tablet and the robot for the Science Fair project – these are all examples of resources.

RISK – Something that *could* happen on your project. It could be good, or bad, but it isn't something that will definitely happen. It might happen, or it might not - which is why we generally assign a *probability* to each risk. This is usually something like "very likely to happen", "likely to happen", "might happen", "probably won't happen", and "not very likely at all". If something is definitely going to happen (100% sure), it is called an *issue*.

Risks also have an *impact*, or how good or bad things could be if the risk happens. If it is a negative (bad) risk, the impact could range from "really bad" to "not really that bad". Note that a positive risk is also called an *opportunity*, which means something *good* might happen - this impact could range from "really good" to "a little bit good".

RUMOR – A story that is being passed around that may not be true, or may be an outright lie. Rumors can be relatively harmless (I heard a rock star is in town!), or may be intended to be hurtful to other people. Don't start rumors. If you don't know if what you heard is really true, don't pass it on!

SCOPE – This is "everything" you are trying to do with your project, which will contribute to building your Work Breakdown Structure. You can start with a high level scope statement like "build a tree house" or "build a haunted house" and then make it more detailed so it is clear to everyone what you are trying to accomplish with your project. For example "build a tree house with enough levels and platforms to hold eight people", or "build a scary haunted house that fits in the garage, basement and back yard".

SEQUENCE – The order in which something occurs compared to another thing. For example, A comes before B, B comes before C in the alphabet – that is a sequence. (A->B->C)

SKILL – Knowing how to do an activity, like climb a tree, tie knots, and so on.

STAKEHOLDER – Anyone who has an interest in, may be affected by, or benefit from the outcomes of your project is called a *Stakeholder*. Every child who could possibly come to the dance was a potential stakeholder, and the principal was a stakeholder because she was the *Project Sponsor* of the dance, and she wanted the dance to be a success.

TARGET DEADLINE – This is when you want a task or even the entire project to be complete. The kids need to have everything ready for the dance by a certain date.

TASK – An assignment or activity to get a specific part of the project completed – like making decorations, choosing the music, selling tickets, etc.

VARIABLES – These are "unknown" things we may need to plan for – like how many people will come to the dance, make decorations or bring baking. We often don't know at the beginning what all of the variables may be, and they can change over time.

VISION – The "big picture idea" of what you are trying to do, whether it is building a tree house, designing an experiment, painting a picture or something else.

WORK BREAKDOWN STRUCTURE – A tree structure diagram, representing the work to be done (deliverables), breaking higher level items into smaller items (more detailed).

Glossary

Notes for Parents and Teachers

This book introduces children to a number of basic project management concepts (or simply *project concepts*, if you prefer).

Resources and Downloads

www.projectkidsadventures.com/resources

School Curriculum Applicability

The concepts covered in this book include independent learning and aspects of technology, specifically:

- Characteristics of technology and technological outcomes.

- Technological modelling, products and systems.

215

- Planning, identifying resources, skills and stages required to complete an outcome.

The relevant school curriculum standards include, at a minimum:

New Zealand

The New Zealand Curriculum (2007)

Alignment to Key Competencies

All five of the key competencies for living and lifelong learning are addressed and demonstrated throughout the story.

- *Thinking* (Project planning, creative solutioning)

- *Using language, symbols and texts* (Project planning, Work Breakdown Structure, Network diagrams)

- *Managing self* (Motivation, resourcefulness, determination to succeed)

- *Relating to others* (Stakeholder engagement, change management, understanding motivation, advocates and antagonists)

- *Participating and contributing* (Working in a project team)

Health and Physical Education

- Relationships with Other People [Level 1,2,3]

    o Relationships

    o Interpersonal skills

Technology

- Nature of Technology [Level 1,2,3]

    o Characteristics of technological outcomes

- Technological Knowledge [Level 1,2,3]

    o Technological modeling

    o Technological systems

- Technological Practice [Level 1,2,3,4]

    o Outcome development and evaluation

Australia

Australian Curriculum [ACARA]

General Capabilities

- Personal & Social Capability

Year 5 & 6 - Health & Physical Education

- ACPPS055 - Practise skills to establish and manage relationships

- ACPPS056 - Examine the influences of emotional responses on behaviour and relationships

- ACPPS057 - Recognise how media and important people in the community influence personal attitudes, beliefs, decisions and behaviours

Year 7 & 8 - Health & Physical Education

- ACPPS074 - Investigate the benefits of relationships and examine their impact on their own and others' health and wellbeing

- ACPPS075 - Analyse factors that influence emotions , and develop strategies to demonstrate empathy and sensitivity

Year 5 & 6 - Technology

- ACTDEP026 - Apply safe procedures when using a variety of materials, components, tools, equipment and techniques to make designed solutions

- ACTDEP028 - Develop project plans that include consideration of resources when making designed solutions individually and collaboratively

Year 7& 8 - Technology

- ACTDEP036 - Generate, develop, test and communicate design ideas, plans and processes for various audiences using appropriate technical terms and technologies including graphical representation techniques

- ACTDEP039 - Use project management processes when working individually and collaboratively to coordinate production of designed solutions

United States

National Standards

Technology

- NT.K-12.1 Basic operations and concepts

- NT.K-12.6 Technology problem-solving and decision-making tools

United Kingdom

Primary Curriculum

Design and Technology Key Stage 1

1. Developing, planning and communicating ideas (a,b,c,d,e)

2. Working with tools, equipment, materials and components to make quality products (a,c,d,e)

3. Evaluating processes and products (a,b)

5. Breadth of study (a,b,c)

Design and Technology Key Stage 2

1. Developing, planning and communicating ideas (a,b,c)

2. Working with tools, equipment, materials and components to make quality products (a,b,d,e)

3. Evaluating processes and products (a,b,c)

4. Knowledge and understanding of materials and components (a,b,c)

5. Breadth of study (a,b,c)

Portugal

Curriculum Goals for Technological Education (5th and 6th grade)

5th Grade

6.1: Record information in a rational and concise manner.

6.2: Interpret and represent information aiming at the organization and ranking of its content.

7.1: Identify technological vocabulary, using it to transmit ideas and opinions.

7.2: Interpret instructions and graphical/technical schemes.

9.1: Organize events in chronological order.

6th Grade

8.1: Identify the required steps to organize and plan tasks (workspace, materials and tools, lists of components, etc.).

10.1: Demonstrate facts and events that show cause and effect relationship.

10.2: Distinguish between a sequence and an aggregate of actions.

13.1: Identify requirements and available resources.

13.2: Develop skills for finding the best solution, assessing pros and cons, and critically evaluating achieved solutions.

Curriculum Goals for Information and Communication Technologies (7th and 8th grade)

(…) prioritize student participation in small projects, problem solving, and practical exercises focused on project/product development.

Project Management Concepts

Amanda's father introduced her to the basic project stages that are common to every successful project, regardless of your preferred terminology or system. These are reinforced in each book.

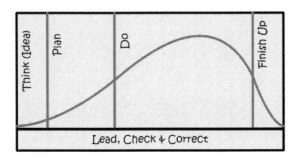

The chapters can also be mapped directly to project phases:

- **Initiation** (Idea / Think)

    o   Hasty Decisions

    o   I Could Have Said No

    o   Pimple Pete

    o   I Plead Insanity

- **Planning** (Plan)

    o   New Recruits

    o   Second Fiddle

    o   Sour Grapes

The Valentine's Day Project *Disaster*

- o Fearless Leader
- o No Man's Land
- o Behind Enemy Lines
- o Battle Plans

- **Execution** (Do)

  - o Because I Said So
  - o Green-Eyed Monster
  - o Rumor Has It…
  - o Poison Pen
  - o One Little Kiss
  - o Face the Music
  - o Love Me…Not

- **Closeout** (Finish Up)

  - o Love Me…Not
  - o Sweet Revenge
  - o Just Desserts

- **Project Control** (Lead, Check & Correct)

  - o Second Fiddle
  - o New Recruits
  - o Sour Grapes

Notes for Parents and Teachers

- ○ Fearless Leader

- ○ No Man's Land

- ○ Battle Plans

- ○ Poison Pen

- ○ Face the Music

Planning

During the planning process the kids do a brainstorming session, followed by development of a simple **Work Breakdown Structure** showing what needs to be done or delivered.

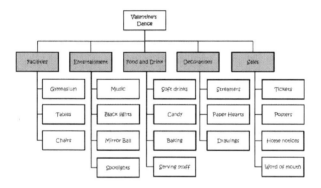

Next, they put the activities into logical sequences, identifying *dependencies* between tasks. This project is similar to the Haunted House, with parallel activity streams. This is represented in a *network diagram* (the children call it a bubble diagram in the story).

The Valentine's Day Project *Disaster*

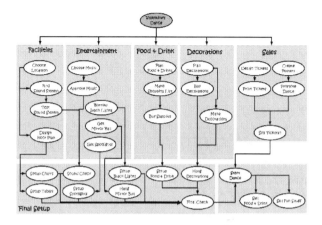

In this network diagram (sometimes called a dependency diagram), it becomes clear what needs to happen first, second and so on, so they can work on the right tasks as the right time and in the right order, while still being prepared for the next activity.

They then use *task estimating* to see if they will be able to complete the project on time, and where the longest chain of task dependencies is; this is called the *critical path*.

Notes for Parents and Teachers

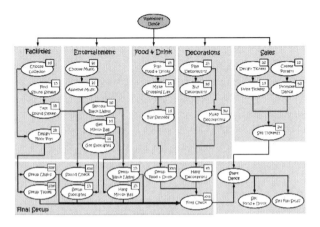

Tim then draws a *Gantt chart* to help visualize and track tasks, which is a planning tool they used on a previous project. The Gantt chart shows tasks, schedule, resources and dependencies all on one combined diagram. A simple Gantt chart can be used effectively for this project, with the groups of tasks, timeframes and who is the lead for each task clearly visible. Arrows show sequencing where it is not immediately obvious (note: drawing all of the dependency arrows would make it quite messy for readability of the Gantt chart the kids are using, so some were omitted).

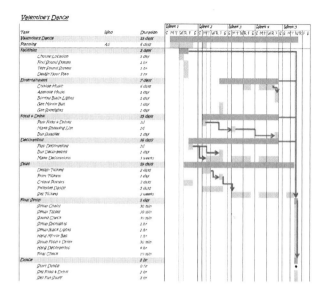

The project has several parallel streams, which in this case worked out so that the grouped tasks can mostly be done independently until the *Final Setup* stage, where everything must be put together just prior to the dance.

Tracking Time

This book also includes a visual timeframe in each chapter (a special calendar with completed dates crossed off, days remaining and an indicator of the current project phase).

This simple, familiar visual is intended to help the children to be more aware of time passing as they progress through the book and the project, and intentionally add a little bit of deadline anxiety - "only 9 days left!" Young or old, we all seem to work better when we have a deadline and have visibility of time elapsing.

Focus on Relationship Management

There is a strong focus on *relationships* (and not just the boy/girl Valentine's kind) in this story. Learning to work with people is a crucial skill in life, and there is an explicit emphasis on relationship, stakeholder and change management aspects and skills development throughout the story.

The glossary has also been significantly expanded from the prior books to include the related concepts and definitions introduced in this book.

In some ways, the organizing of the dance itself is simpler than some of their other projects - at least, from the technical perspective of identifying the deliverables and putting together a plan.

- Have it in the school Gymnasium? Check.

- Food and Drinks? Check.

- Music? Check.

- Tickets and flyers? Check.

- Decorations? Check.

- Participants? *Uh oh...*

The project kids are forced to learn a whole range of 'soft' skills and terms in order to 'survive' this project and deliver a successful dance. These skills are centered around working with people, influencing them, and engaging some very special people (*advocates*) to help convince everybody to come to the dance. Not *only* come to the dance, but to make decorations and bring baking, and therefore help out (for free!) and make the project easier as well.

Challenges

The primary obstacle facing the project kids is the extreme lack of interest in the dance (not apathy, but an active disinterest), due to the spectacular failure of the dance the prior year. They recognized that although they could technically organize a 'dance', there was a very high risk that there would be negligible participation. This introduced secondary, but significant risks in relation to the

Notes for Parents and Teachers

project budget (expenditures for food that would be wasted, and low income/cost recovery for what is supposed to be a fundraiser for the school).

The kids arrive at some very creative solutions that (if they worked) would reduce the cost risk and risk of food waste, through the contest for best baking - while hopefully raising interest (motivation) to come to the dance and see if they won. A second idea was intended to reduce the workload of the committee, while also raising the interest levels of students, through having students create and hang up decorations which would be judged. Both ideas use the concept of *crowdsourcing*.

Unfortunately, the principal pointed out that while these ideas both had merit, they were not likely to be strong enough motivators on their own to (a) get kids to come, (b) make decorations, or (c) bring baking.

The project kids needed to learn a whole new set of 'soft skills' and concepts in order to tackle these obstacles, including:

- Stakeholder management (who are they, how we engage with them, managing expectations, etc.)

- Relationship management (how to get along with different kinds of people)

- Influencing the actions and behaviours of others

- Understanding motivational factors (Extrinsic & Intrinsic)

- Additional communication skills and approaches (we can always get better at this, no matter how old we are)

- Utilizing **Advocates** to introduce positive changes and communicate effectively to the masses, while increasing stakeholder motivation and engagement.

They also learned more about leadership (delegation, responsibility and accountability).

Unfortunately, they had other problems as well, from a simple misunderstanding about a little kiss, to...

Subversive Forces

The kids also have to work against 'subversive forces', in the form of the grade 8 bully 'Pimple Pete', who ran the unsuccessful dance the year before. A reluctant provider of information about the prior year's dance, Pete works to continually undermine the efforts of the dance project team. This first act takes the form of 'telling the principal' when the girls are forced to enlist the other Project Kids from the Primary school, because the perception of the dance is so extremely negative they can get no help from students in the Middle School.

When he is unsuccessful in trying to gain control of the dance (and worse - the Primary school kids are now allowed to help *organize* the dance!), Peter resorts to viral communication in the form of malicious **rumors** that are intended to make the dance committee give up hope (No more decorations! No baking!). However, the rumors also get quite personal as one of the messages seeks to undermine the relationship between a project team member and a key advocate. The bully, Peter, attacks from all fronts - using a negative form of 'advocacy' to spread his rumors. (This highlights the importance and moral values of being careful with all of your messages, as dishonest messages can spread as quickly - often more so - than real, honest messages).

Driven 'underground' with his activities following the principal's speech about rumors, we see and hear very little from Pimple Pete - until the final, very public act of sabotage.

With the support of the principal (their Project Sponsor), a store of innate stubbornness and a lot of ingenuity, the project kids are able to recover from each of these near-disastrous acts of sabotage and keep the project moving forward.

Other concepts

A number of common project concepts are also introduced, either directly or indirectly in the story, including:

- **Change Management** (Battle Plans / Because I Said So / Rumor Has It... / Poison Pen / Sweet Revenge)

The Valentine's Day Project *Disaster*

- **Cost / Budget** (Behind Enemy Lines)

- **Estimating / Measurement** (Behind Enemy Lines, Rumor Has It...)

- **Leadership** (Fearless Leader, Face the Music)

- **Lessons Learned** (Just Desserts)

- **Requirements** (New Recruits, Battle Plans)

- **Resource Management** (Behind Enemy Lines)

- **Risk Management** (Behind Enemy Lines, Rumor Has It... / Sweet Revenge)

- **Stakeholder Management** (Pimple Pete / No-Man's Land / Behind Enemy Lines / Battle Plans / Because I Said So / One Little Kiss / Love Me...Not)

- **Teamwork / Human Resource Management** (Hasty Decisions / I Could Have Said No / I Plead Insanity / New Recruits / Sour Grapes / Fearless Leader / Behind Enemy Lines / Green-Eyed Monster / Face the Music)

Other Educational Resources

There are an increasing number of resources being developed to support Project Management education in schools, covering Grades 1-12 and beyond.

If you are an educator, some resources I recommend you take a look at are:

Project-Based Learning for Students Ages 13-19, a non-profit program offered by the PMI Education Foundation (www.pmi.org/pmief).

Projects From the Future, a training kit for teachers to help them teach project concepts in the classroom (Primary and higher). The kit was developed by the PMI Northern Italy Chapter (www.pmi-nic.org), and is also available through the PMI Education Foundation.

A picture book that teaches project concepts for younger children (ages 6-8) is Before the Snow Flies: Lando Banager's Tales of a Woodland Project Manager by Ira A. Seiken, PMP.

And of course, please read the other books in the Project Kids Adventures series!

If you come across other useful resources for developing Life Skills through Project Management, please send me an email at gary.nelson@gazzasguides.com.

About the Author

Gary M. Nelson, PMP (Gazza) is a Project Manager and father of three boys. Gary has worked on projects in New Zealand, Taiwan, Hong Kong, the US and Canada since 1989. He is also the author of **Gazza's Guide to Practical Project Management**, which uses experience-based stories for grown-up children (i.e. adults) to share project lessons.

Gary's first three children's books in the Project Kids Adventures series are **The Ultimate Tree House Project**, **The Scariest Haunted House Project - *Ever!*** and *The Amazing Science Fair Project*.

About the Illustrator

My name is Mathew Frauenstein. Amongst other things I enjoy drawing and gaming, so these activities tend to take up most of my free time. However, when I am not doing either of those I will be sleeping, eating or sitting through another day of that horrid activity known as school. At the time of writing this stanza I am living in New Zealand, a very green country known for its friendly natives and its endangered national bird the Kiwi (sadly it cannot fly). However I have not always lived in New Zealand, but rather I was born in South Africa, where the first four years of my life were spent doing what babies normally do: eating, crying, sleeping and filling their diapers with gifts for their parents.

Other Books

Project Management (Adult/Bigger Kids)

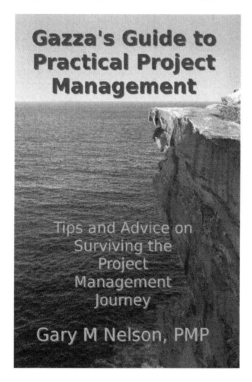

Gazza's Guide to Practical Project Management

Available in Paperback & eBook formats

Print ISBN 978-1478345046, 272 pages

Project Kids Adventures

Project Kids Adventures Series

#1 – The Ultimate Tree House Project

#2 – The *Scariest* Haunted House Project – *Ever!*

#3 - The Amazing Science Fair Project

#4 - The Valentine's Day Project Disaster

Coming Soon

#5 - The Easter Bully Transformation Project

Social Stuff

Series Website: www.projectkidsadventures.com

Facebook: TheValentinesDayProjectDisaster

Twitter: @ProjectKidsAdv

Google+: +Projectkidsadventures

YouTube: ProjectKidsAdventure channel

Email: projectkids@gazzasguides.com

10570005R00146

Printed in Germany
by Amazon Distribution
GmbH, Leipzig